Jobs for a Wet Day

Ger Reidy

JOBS FOR A WET DAY

JOBS FOR A WET DAY

is published in 2015 by
ARLEN HOUSE
42 Grange Abbey Road
Baldoyle
Dublin 13
Ireland
Phone/Fax: 353 86 8207617
Email: arlenhouse@gmail.com

Distributed internationally by
SYRACUSE UNIVERSITY PRESS
621 Skytop Road, Suite 110
Syracuse, NY 13244–5290
Phone: 315–443–5534/Fax: 315–443–5545
Email: supress@syr.edu

978–1–85132–139–1, paperback

© Ger Reidy, 2015

The moral rights of the author have been asserted

Typesetting by Arlen House

Cover artwork by Dermot Seymour

Jobs for a Wet Day has received financial assistance from the Arts Council under the Publications/Title by Title Scheme

Contents

11   Nobody Knows

27   Headage

41   My Big Day

53   Seventeen and a Half Minutes

65   Jobs for a Wet Day

79   You Do Know Who I Am?

91   Snow

101   The Visit

113   The Buck at the End of the Road

129   Argentina

141   At the Crossroads

151   The Gentlemen

164   *About the Author*
       Acknowledgements

For my grandson Marcin Reidy
who for me makes this absurd rock go around the sun

Jobs for a Wet Day

Nobody Knows

Sometimes I think that I live in a strange village. It happens when I'm on my fourth or fifth pint. Nothing strange about that. Most middle-aged men have what you might call a fleeting moment of clarity that hits them from nowhere when the talking stops for no reason and they catch sight of themselves in the bar mirror. In my case it only happens in this watering hole, because my daughter works here. She doesn't know who I am, that I'm her father I mean. Here is the only place I can see her, but tonight it could all come to a head. It has to sometime.

They're a sound crowd in the pub all the same, sure I'd be lost without them. We all have names. They call me Red, on account of my hair and because I paint all the hay sheds in the parish red. Then there's Lightning Johnny, who never got out of bed before midday, and The Contender who always picks a fight on Paddy's Day and gets hammered. They have a name on my daughter. She's red too – it's as if they know – The Red Hot Chilli Pepper, but they've shortened it to the Chilli Pepper on account of her mood swings.

She's a bit wild at times, she always has the young fellas eating out of her hand. The way she dresses doesn't help. It's hard to watch sometimes, the way they leer at her, even the old bucks have no shame. I suppose that's why I'm down here most nights to try and protect her. That got me into trouble one night when she threw me out.

'I'm well able to mind myself', she snarled bitterly. 'I had to learn early, so don't be acting like a father. You should be at home minding your own family'.

I suppose she's right. I've been ignoring the wife lately and Paul, my son. He was twenty-one yesterday. We're having a splash here tonight in the pub for him. He likes a drink too, but he's not a real drinker, he just buys them cans in Aldi and sucks them in the flat in Galway. I'd prefer to see him out mixing with real people instead of playing some game on the computer in the flat or trying to chat up some young one on that bloody screen, but sure with the drink driving laws now everyone's afraid. I find it tricky enough myself going home. I take a back road through the wood but sure even that's not safe.

He's in his last year in the GMIT college doing Construction Studies – he'll have no bother getting a job, he'll be off my payroll then. He comes home the odd weekend and we have a pint in the village, but he has nothing to say. I can't knock any talk out of him. He had his eye on Maria, that's the daughter, the last time too. Jesus, life is never simple. Some days I think everyone knows, especially after drink, and other days I think sure they can't know, or if they did somebody would say something. I can't talk to anyone about it, that's the worst part. So I normally convince myself that nobody knows and then I try to convince myself that it didn't happen, until I go for a pint and I see Maria and her mother talking to me through her.

Maria has another pint in front of me, she fills them just at the right time. Fr Pat is great though – he got us all on a

FÁS scheme, working every second week cleaning up the village. The place is looking well even though the bank, the post office and the school are all closed down. There's only the pub and the church left and they too are losing customers. When a village loses the school it takes the heart out of the place. They're bussed into town now and they call it progress. The bank allowed us to paint the place this year and put flower boxes on the windowsills. It makes all the difference to the square, if only we could get the County Council to paint the courthouse.

On my week off I keep an eye on the farm. I used to send milk to the creamery but sure there's no money in it so I quit last year and let the calves do the milking. The young fella shows no interest so why would I be killing myself getting up in the dark to get a slap of a shitty tail on the lug? The missus has a good job now, she done that assertiveness night class course in Castlebar. She earns more than I do on the FÁS and the land put together, working in what she calls Human Resources with some American crowd that make artificial hips. She talks a lot about motivation and going forward. I think if she was in reverse these days she'd still be going forward. She's certainly not backward. It's people skills and the importance of communication – when she starts that kind of talk I get dizzy and I have to head down the land to clear my head or go to the pub. The priest even wants her to give a talk in the community centre as part of the festival about modern living in a rural village entitled 'Communities Going Forward in Challenging Times: Working Together as a Team'.

Anyway she's changed a lot in the last few years, she's not the woman I married. Maybe I've changed too, she's probably saying the same about me. We've plenty of money now, she's even on about buying a flat in Marbella. Sure what would we do out there? Golf is her new discovery and there's nothing but brochures and property supplements about Spain all over the house. She wants to change the car too, wants to buy one of those open top yokes – they'd never keep the water out after the seals went but try explaining that to her. She met this lady at the assertiveness course a year ago and it's like she's different. She dresses up a lot, more than before, even going shopping. Sometimes I think she's ashamed of me when she introduces me to her new friends who are all from the right side of town. She never comes to the pub anymore even though she got on really well with Maria. Sometimes I think she knows, but has decided to say nothing. They even went shopping to Galway once where she introduced her to Paul – Jesus, life gets complicated. Sometimes the pressure is too much. If I couldn't get down the land to clear my head, I think I'd throw a rope over the beam in the hayshed and call it a day.

It's great down the land away from the racket. I sit on a rock on top of a rushy hill and smoke two Majors looking at Croagh Patrick. It must be twenty miles away but it always takes my mind off things when I go there – ever since I was a child and there was trouble in the house, when the old fella fell in drunk. What was St Patrick at up there? He must have had a lot of short circuits in the fuse box, or maybe he was trying to achieve closure, as my wife would say? I'd nearly try it myself, if I had a few crates of Heineken and a few boxes of Majors. I might find some answers or at least the questions, but here in this fog I can't see anything.

They'll all be in soon now for the party and Maria's on for the full night. 'Same again', I say to Maria and a drop of anti-freeze from the top shelf. I wish this night was over. We bought Paul a laptop, the wife got it at the sales last January, but sure they're cheaper now. It's all wrapped up beside the stage. The band is the usual clot of country and western leprechauns who were has-beens before they started. Their CD is flogged on local radio and they've even been to Nashville. Since then they whine in a Mayo-Tennessee accent, wear white suits, cowboy hats and have a huge middle-aged female audience. Their delivery is as subtle as a grey crow landing on a dung pit. They're costing me a thousand euros.

'Hello Red', they say as the place fills up.

Maria is dolled up more than usual and has another pint and a short out on the counter before I know it. I'll try to stay fairly sober tonight. The wife is coming here after some rural development committee meeting and Paul is supposed to be here around ten, if he leaves the pub in town on time. He's into rock music since we got him that electric guitar for his eighteenth. I suppose there's nothing wrong with that as long as he keeps his eye on the ball. He plays in this band, they tell me he's good. Sure I can't listen to that noisy racket, give me a bit of Willie Nelson or Hank Williams. The sandwiches are covered in foil and sitting on trays inside the bar and I have the barbecue ready for the sausages and burgers.

Maria has stopped talking to her mother Bernie. It seems they fell out around the time the missus introduced Maria to Paul. Maria moved out around then into a flat in town and has had a trail of boyfriends since. She's been drinking a lot too, she's changed. It seems that she's interested in Paul again, cut the hair up short and became even more reckless. I doubt if her mother told her anything but I don't know. I'll have to meet her some day to try and find out what she's said to Maria.

Bernie is a nice person. I knew her from school days. She's very bright and the parents had big plans for her. Her brothers and sisters have all done well. You'd often see her brothers mentioned in the property supplement in the *Irish Independent*. Two of them started as block-layers up in Dublin and sure now they own three pubs and have fifty men working under them on sites. They come down a few times a year driving bigger cars each time. One of them has the latest Merc. The rest of them are teachers and one is a doctor. Bernie's parents are still alive but you never see them out anymore except at mass. They have a two-storey house with two big monkey puzzle trees on either side of a long driveway and a Virginia creeper covering the gable.

We were going out for three years when it happened. We had planned to get married. The night after Mayo won the Connacht Final we had a few drinks on us, and going home in the Cortina she insisted I pull in at the bend where the council dumps the tar barrels.

'It's safe', she demanded. 'We're using the rhythm method. Remember they showed us on the chart in the pre-marriage course the night Fr Jack tiptoed out of the room'.

That chart looked like some kind of board game to me like the Ludo we played when we were kids. I didn't argue but I wasn't too comfortable about the whole thing.

We were getting on well then, four months away from the big day. We had picked a site that my father gave us on top of the hill overlooking a lake and had chosen a house plan from Bungalow Bliss for a dormer bungalow. Her brothers would do the block-laying and my uncle would do the plumbing. I'd do all the ground works and build the septic tank.

Anyway she got a bit nervous the following month and everything was put on hold. Then after the second month she called it off. It seems her parents couldn't handle the shame. My parents were furious and took offence that I wasn't good enough for her. She had to take sides with her crowd and we had to stop seeing each other. It was unbearable.

I called down one night after a few pints. She met me at the door and bundled me into the garden.

'I'm taking the boat on Thursday', she said.

I found out afterwards that her parents gave her the return fare, organised the clinic and her uncle would put her up for a week. I couldn't handle that type of thing. For me it all starts at conception and after that it's all progression until the final whistle. Anyway I went to England with her to try and persuade her to see sense.

She was awful sick on the boat bobbing around on the Irish Sea in a gale all night. There was sick everywhere, they couldn't get the smell of it out of the carpets. It took her a day to recover in Holyhead where we had to stay in a boarding house for the night. God, I remember looking out the window at the gulls and the smell of salt everywhere and trucks waiting in patient lines for the delayed ferries. After we got the train to London she slept for almost fifteen hours at her uncle's, while I crashed on the floor of Johnny Riley's flat in Harrow.

There was nothing between us now, all those nights in the Royal Ballroom, all those Sundays spent in the old Cortina going to the beach or football matches all over Connacht with my father, who was proud at the thought of having a teacher in the family, evaporated. There was only the clinic at three. Bernie could have done any job, she didn't have to depend on the priest and the national teaching. After three hours I hoped that I had persuaded her to keep it. I told her I'd support her and pay for the education. I told her that I loved her and I'm not one for that class of talk. Maybe that was what she wanted to hear, but it was too late now. We went to the clinic at three. I stayed outside praying the few prayers left in my skull. She came out soon afterwards holding these tablets, crying, shaking all over, before she screamed and threw them in my face.

'They wouldn't give a refund', she sobbed after a long time. I didn't care a damn about the bloody refund. I tried to put my arm around her, but she was having none of it.

'Christ', I said. 'Can't we be friends at least?'

I never felt so lonely. Walking around London with four days to kill, waiting for the return ticket and pretending to her uncle that everything went according to plan. We went to the sights, Trafalgar Square, the Tower of London. We even took a boat down the river to see the Cutty Sark but it was useless – she wouldn't thaw. I took to drink on the last day. I've never gone to London since.

Anyway, speaking of herself, she was born seven pounds four ounces, or so they told me in the local shop – 'red curly hair, a bit like your own'. They made a point of telling me that. Some days I'd think nobody knows and other days I'd think sure they all know. We agreed not to see each other after London. She got a job in Dublin, the brothers set her up in the building company doing accounts. She wasn't seen around for five years until the father got sick. Then she moved down and put Maria in the local school. There are times when I think I still love her. I suppose I can't admit that to myself or that would cause more trouble. Anyway it's too late now. She was so bright and witty but she lost all that. Now it's just a cloudy face that greets me when I meet her outside mass. What a waste, what a stupid senseless waste. It makes me very angry. If times were like they are now we'd be together, all three of us, but respect got in the way.

The place is filling up nicely and the sandwiches and cocktail sausages will soon be out. I see Paul coming in the door, a bit tipsy, with his friends. By now the band has started wailing out some Charlie Pride song. I'm not drunk but I'm not sober. I welcome Paul and point to the presents.

'You're a popular young fella', I say.

'Yeah Da', he says and brushes me off. 'And how's the hottest thing within a hundred mile radius?' he croons at Maria and sweeps towards the bar.

I order more drink off Maria to distract her. In fact I order drink for everyone in the bar. Paul looks up at the band and the singer winks back. I'm hoping he won't give him the fingers. I don't want trouble, all I want is a quiet life, but that's too much to ask I suppose.

The wife and her golfing friends from town announce their arrival. She is introducing Paul to them but she doesn't seem to see me. They keep to themselves. Paul has a lot of friends here and there seems to be loads of Maria's friends too for some reason. Maria has left the bar and is gathering glasses. Paul is introducing Maria to my wife's cronies.

I can't let the whole thing escalate, but Jesus, what am I going to do? I interrupt the band and ask them would they let Paul play for a while. They agree and they call upon him to join in on the lead guitar. I can see he's angry, but his mother cheers him up onto the stage. It gives me a chance to talk to Maria but what am I going to say? I didn't think he could play, the state he was in, but he managed to clamber onto the stage.

'Ever heard of Led Zepp?' he growled.

'Go for it', his friends shouted.

'This is called *Whole Lotta Love*', and he dedicates it to Maria. The band don't seem to be able to join in so he grabs the mike and takes over the stage. I can see Maria is impressed. I can't handle the tension. I should have sorted all this mess out before now but I'm not one for confrontation. It's all going to come to a head tonight. I can see it now. I steady myself and decide to ring Bernie. I kept her number just in case anything happened to Maria. I'm not supposed to have her number – I got it off Maria one night when she left her wallet on the counter.

I ring Bernie, her mother answers. It was a long time since I heard that voice, memories come flooding back. It hadn't changed since we were engaged, still cold and frail. I freeze and cut her off. I ring again. When Bernie answers I apologise for calling so she wouldn't hang up.

'It's an emergency', I insist and plead with her not to leave the phone down. I keep talking about Maria and Paul and how we have to stop it. It's hard to hear anything with the racket in the pub. There is still no response from her. 'Please', I beg. Then the phone goes dead.

The food is circulating now. Paul is still beating the guitar and his mates are singing along with him. When he finishes there is huge applause. He can play the thing alright. It's strange how you notice things sometimes when you have a few pints. I guess I haven't noticed him much lately. Where do the years go? Here I am looking across at my wife and sure a stranger would never know we were, I mean are, an item. She never even looked my way all night. It's hard to know when things die between people. We never have arguments, it's like we stay out of each other's way. We never do anything together. All I know is that it's dead as far as I'm concerned, but it's hard to admit to that too. Sure I can live with that if I could get over tonight. Paul is still on the stage. His crowd are shouting 'Led Zepp, Led Zepp', and my wife is presenting him with our present.

'I have an announcement to make', Paul shouts.

'Not yet', Maria shouts back.

Then Paul blows a kiss over the bar and wades in with a few phrases thanking his mother.

'I have an announcement to make', he insists and he calls over Maria.

I can't believe this is happening. It's like you've been told that you're terminally ill, but this is supposed to happen to other people.

'This lady and I have some news', he declares to everybody.

My wife seems to be thrilled and everyone gapes at the stage. They all seem to be happy. It's only now after all these years I discover that nobody knows. How could it have been a secret?

'This lady', my son goes on, 'and I would formally like to announce our engagement'.

There are great cheers and hugs all around, nobody hugs me, it's like I have become invisible. I don't know where to disappear to when I see Bernie coming in the door, my heart is jumping in my chest.

'Congratulations', they hug her.

'How did you know, Mum?' Maria calls her up onto the stage, but Bernie isn't smiling.

'I've got an announcement to make too', Bernie says.

She stuns the pub. She was never one to be in the limelight but now she is a teacher again and we are her pupils. My knees are shaking. The place is silent except for the machine washing the glasses.

'I've been living a lie for twenty-four years', she proclaims solemnly. 'Ireland has changed a lot since then. There were no choices back in 1982. If it was now I'd have had a life. You might wonder why I'm talking tonight, well it's to do with Maria, or more to the point, her father'.

Everyone looks at me and then I wonder sure they must have known all along or was it because I was the only one left at the bar.

'I have done him a great wrong, he's a gentleman. I left this village before Maria was born, I had to before they sacked me. Those of you old enough know that I had plans to live with a local man. I made a great mistake, I should have listened to him. Anyway he is Maria's Dad'.

I could feel all the eyes on me now, the silence terrible and sweat running off me. My wife and her friends burst out the door.

'I should have allowed him see his daughter', she went on, 'and involved him in all the decisions made as she was growing up. Instead he's had to come down here every night to see her. I have been very cruel. I want to apologise to Maria and Paul for blighting their night and to ask Joe' – that's me – 'for forgiveness'.

I feel as if a great load has fallen off my shoulders. I find myself crying. I'm so ashamed, I haven't cried since my mother was buried.

'Are ya alright there, Red?' they ask.

I look over at Maria and she runs towards me and slaps me on the face.

'Red, how could you be such a coward living a lie all these years, watching me grow up without a father? Now it's too late Red. All you and mother can do is ruin my only chance at happiness'.

She storms out of the pub with Bernie after her. Paul at this stage has gone missing. I'm worried about him. I track him down in the nettles beside the barbecue.

'I'm sorry son', I say.

He hits me and lands me on top of the cocktail sausages.

'Mam was right', he shouts. 'You're just the village loser'.

I get up and grab him by the shirt and want to say this loser has sacrificed his best years to make a home for and educate an ungrateful punk who's going to have to paddle his own boat from now on, but I don't. I just hold him really tight six inches above the ground by the lapels and let him go. He kicks the barbeque into the nettles, swings again at me before heading out across the village fair green.

At this stage the pub has cleared. Bernie and Maria are having a stiff drink. I enter sheepishly.

'It had to be done', Bernie says. Maria is wilting with tears. 'We couldn't go on living a great lie'.

Maria has her arm around her mother. I sit down a distance from them. They ignore me for a while but I stay. Maria is still sobbing in her mother's arms. I cross the floor in front of them to the bar to grab my pint.

'You better sit down here now', Bernie is firm.

I feel a huge joy, as if everything is possible again, as if I can start living. I cautiously sit near her.

'Here', she insists and I sit beside her. She puts her hand on mine and looks at me. I risk looking at her. Her eyes are welling up. Maria leaves. I look away again. Then the sadness overwhelms me. It comes from nowhere. It's as if all the pain I had for twenty-four years has been converted to sadness. I want to cry but I suddenly feel cold. I can't trust all this now. How am I supposed to believe that everything is going to be alright because now Bernie has decided it is going to be alright? I pull away my hand from hers and fire the glass against the wall. I don't know what to think, I don't know what I'm supposed to feel. I want to believe it will work out this time, but I can't feel anything. I won't let myself feel or maybe I can't feel anything anymore.

Maria comes back. She holds her arms out, then she turns them into fists.

'Fuck you Red, could you not see me bleeding all these years in front of your bloodshot eyes? I've only one thing to say to you, sad, village loser'. She poked me across the chest with her fist on each accusation. 'Only one thing Red, you're twenty-four fucking years late'.

She stormed towards the exit.

'It's ok Red', Bernie reassures me as I leave for the lounge. 'She'll calm down, she needs time'.

Bernie runs after Maria and catches her before she leaves. She's still crying.

'I'm sorry for being a bitch to you all those years', she hugs her mother.

'It's ok love', Bernie reassures her, 'it can't have been easy for you either'.

'What about you and Paul?' Bernie asks. 'You must be angry'.

'I am mum', she says. 'but they say you must find your father before you find a husband according to the psycho books. That fucking Red, I want to break a pint glass into his bloated pimply face, that fucking coward', her voice fills the empty bar.

Bernie comes back into the singing lounge.

'I'll drop her home and be back in five minutes', she whispers to me as if we were married for twenty-five years.

I look around the pub, empty now, the owner left it to Maria for the weekend. I could rob the till but it means nothing to me. I'm beginning to feel a strange happiness come over me while I'm waiting for Bernie to return, like something has lifted. To think that I have a wife and a family seems alien. Everything is different. I help Bernie to lock up and we leave the place in a total mess. We're all red-eyed and washed out. I offer to leave her home but Bernie won't hear of it.

'I'll drop you home', she says. 'I'm sober after this night, that's one thing I'm sure of'.

I hop into Bernie's Peugeot with the *Woman's Way*. The purple dawn is caressing the mountain peaks and the fog along the river seems magical. I haven't noticed that type of thing for years. Bernie looks at me every few minutes as if I'm going to disappear. Maguire's sheep are in my meadow but it doesn't bother me. I'm beginning to feel as if someone cares for me sitting in the passenger seat being driven home.

'There's great suspension in these Peugeots', I say to Bernie, to make sure she hasn't changed her mind about me, trying to make her talk as we cross the humpback bridge. She laughs.

'Do you remember the first time you said that to me?'

I had forgotten. She laughs again. Bernie was always a great one for the Peugeots.

'What a chat-up line'.

We're laughing as she pulls in outside the house.

'Well now you're home safe', Bernie says cheerfully.

But something else is dawning on me too as the Peugeot goes out of sight and I'm leaning against the garden wall looking up at that crack in the chimney, smoking a Major.

Where is home?

Headage

It was the postman turning his white van in a big exaggerated sweep in the gravelled yard which woke up Gaughan. The wind had gone south and sheets of rain were spraying onto the front of the house. Gaughan stretched himself and stumbled slowly in his vest and long johns to the hall. He checked the letterbox, but nothing again today except a notice about a toy sale in Quinns and a letter from the African Missions for his dead mother. It was almost twelve o'clock on a Monday morning and November was threshing the last leaves off the trees. How would he find out when the check was due? He turned on the television to see if there was any news about the headage cheque but he could only see John Wayne being attacked by Apaches on RTÉ1 and Darina Allen cooking a Christmas cake on RTÉ2.

He decided to go to the village. There might be some news in *The Farmers' Journal*. He pulled on the oilskins and pumped the back wheel of the bike – he had a slow puncture that he never got around to fixing. The wind was so strong behind him that all he had to do was sit on the saddle. He hoped the front brake would hold him when he got to the pub as he rounded the bends down the hill, avoiding the whitethorns and fuchsia branches. When he got to the village he dug his wellington into the tar to slow himself down but it was useless and he ended up crashing into the wall of the church. When he straightened himself he looked back at the bike with contempt, saw that the back wheel was bent, glared at it again and flung it into the river. He was talking to himself now:

'What a start to the week', he mumbled as he wandered up to the pub.

It was twelve now – Angelus time – and the new young priest had installed an electronic bell in the belfry. All the dogs within a mile radius howled as it went off and Gaughan, suffering from a hangover, quickened his step now in order to get shelter from it in the pub. There were six bikes and several tractors outside.

'It's a day for the high stool', he proclaimed to the crowd in the bar.

They could hardly see who it was at first before he loosened the twine of the hood which was fastened through the lapels of the oilskin between his lips.

'Who's in there?', the barman Ward laughed.

'Pour me a pint, you dopey ass, fast'.

Gaughan eventually zipped himself free and released a small cloud of vapour as he settled himself up on a stool, the water running off the corners of his jacket onto the tiled floor in two pools.

'Put it on the slate', he ordered.

The smoky pub was in full swing, there was even a game of darts started. Gaughan took a copy of *The Farmers' Journal* from the shop. There was a pull-out supplement on deer farming. He read the paper again – nothing about sheep except the price of hoggets in Balltinglass.

'Does anybody know anything about the fucking headage cheque?' he demanded from Ward.

'You're not the first to ask', he replied. 'We're going to ring up after dinner when the office opens in Castlebar'.

'I have to pay the Co-op for wire or they won't give me nuts for the sheep and I badly need a battery for the tractor. Jesus it's no good getting the cheque on Christmas Eve', he said to Reilly, parked up beside him, who was on whiskey. 'It's a bit early for the top shelf Tom?' he asked Reilly but all he said was:

'Them cunts in them offices'.

'Who's going to talk to the crowd in Castlebar?' he asked Ward.

'We were hoping you might', came the reply.

'You need a smooth talker. I'll get the wrong answer'.

'Being nice to them crowd in them offices is no good, we tried that before and it's a waste of time', said another.

'I need another pint so', laughed Gaughan, 'to gather my thoughts'.

The television was on now.

Jesus it's raining all over the world', said Quinn, 'even in China'.

'Put on the country music channel instead of that CNN', said Maguire.

'There's nobody messing with the channels now', said Ward.

'See the notice? We had a row about that last week and there's still two men barred'.

'Who's fucking barred?' demanded Gaughan.

'Never mind, there's men barred and they'll stay barred'.

'In this weather to bar a man is a fucking crime, anyway that CNN is just a big advertisement for itself and America. If you believed them you'd think that they bet the Germans when in fact they only showed up for the photograph. Uncle Joe was the man who took them on in Stalingrad'.

'No, that's where you're wrong', said Quinn. 'It was the Russian winter that beat Hitler and it beat Napoleon before him'.

'Now, now', said Ward. 'There'll be no politics here. That got us into trouble before too'.

'So what are we allowed to talk about? The weather in China?'

'Say nothing about them Germans. Isn't it them that pays the headage?' said Reilly.

'All Germans are nice people', said Gaughan, winking at Ward. 'Did you ever meet one of them?' he asked Kavanagh.

'I did', he said, 'didn't one of them buy an old barn off my neighbour out in the middle of the bog. He gave big money for it too. There's no road into it. He stayed there a couple of years but I don't see him much lately. He put up a big fence about ten foot high around the shack with signs saying "Private! Keep Out". He was some class of an artist I think'.

'Had he a woman?'

'Oh he had, a Fraulein came here looking for him and I think he went to Hamburg to meet her a few times a year. He had a few Alsatians inside barking day and night. No one went near him, even the postman was afraid to go out there'.

'They're not all like that', said Kavanagh. 'There's a buck in town and he's more like a Paddy than a German. He can fix anything and he's big into Christy Moore, in fact I think he plays the bodhran'.

The afternoon wore on as the smoke-filled bar became louder. The mud fell onto the floor off the soles of wellingtons in perfect z's and h's depending on the brand. The barman said 'you might be right' or 'that's the way' or 'it takes all types' as the occasion required. Sometimes the counter was struck if a dispute arose about who played centre back for Mayo in the '51 team. Another could name all the English team that won the World Cup in '66. Someone enquired why there was no grant for spraying rushes, but someone else insisted that a grant for spreading lime would get rid of the rushes. The dogs looked up for gestures that they might receive crisps or chocolate or their owners were having one for the road.

Outside the wind had weakened a little but the rain was heavier. The river was filling with a brown flood coming from the mountain. The light too was fading as the children got off the school bus and walked individually to their houses. Lights were coming on in some houses as the women prepared for the children, other houses were dark waiting for someone to come home and claim them. The teacher passed over the bridge and the council workers on a dumper went the other way filling potholes. A tractor with silage in a transport box stopped outside the shop for diesel, a blue rope and two dogs trailing after it.

'Did anyone ring them crowd in the office in Castlebar?' Reilly asked.

'I'll ring them, you leave it to me', Gaughan insisted.

Ward gave him the coins for the phone box beside the dart board.

'Hello', Gaughan was shouting at the phone as it was ringing. The bar went silent.

'It's the headage he's ringing up about', someone whispered.

'Thank you for calling', the voice said. 'All our operators are busy, please hold'.

'Hello', shouted Gaughan, not knowing that it was prerecorded. 'More fifty pences, we're running low'.

'Your call is being dealt with in strict rotation', came the voice.

'Hold on, quiet, she'll be on in a minute, more coins', Gaughan demanded. The bar remained silent when the voice said.

'If you want to contact the severely disadvantaged area section press 1, to contact farm modernisation grants press 2, to contact the beef premium section press 3, to contact the forestry grant aid section press 4, to contact the slaughter premium section press 5, otherwise please hold'. Then it all started again after one minute.

'All our operators are …' the voice went on. After about twenty minutes Gaughan thumped the phone.

'They're gone home now', said Ward, 'sure they finish over there around three'.

'Them cunts in them fucking offices', said Reilly, 'you'd think it was their own money'.

'I'm going to be down here first thing tomorrow at eleven and that's the first thing I'll do', said Gaughan.

A faint watery sunlight rose over the graveyard hill and angled itself across the floor as the last of the rain retreated east. These last sunrays fell on the sheep dogs under the dart board licking their genitals. It crawled perceptively up the floral wallpaper and eventually expired at the calendar that proclaimed Thomas Walsh prime beef, pork and lamb.

The few that left the pub were replaced by bachelors as they settled in until closing time. Some of them didn't talk, just stared at a spot on the wall in some Zen-like pose and every now and again would grunt or lift their glasses off the counter for a refill. Some nights there were four of them in a row beside each other, raising eyebrows, nodding or smiling.

Other nights when the mime broke down they excelled in minimalism. One might utter 'grey crows' or after a half an hour 'limestone land', another 'de Valera' or' rushes'. Of the six or eight words falling out of their mouths like lead ball bearings, rushes always featured. It seemed to unify them with a profound sense of discovery as if their lives could be condensed into their success or failure in the ground war against rushes. Then they would all say 'rushes' together several times sampling the word at different levels before allowing the acknowledgement to arrive and the gravity of the concept bed deep into their consciousness and silence them usually for the remainder of the night. The dogs knew too the rushes moment and would raise one ear before their eyes glazed over again.

Gaughan and Reilly by now would have run out of words too and occupied a hazy no-man's land before Ward called time. They nearly always left together.

'You can be home with me on the tractor', Reilly offered.

They both did some solitary shopping – rashers, sausages, bread and a six pack. Reilly bought a small bottle of Power's whiskey.

'Have you any milk?' Gaughan enquired.

'Only the low-fat', the barman confirmed.

'That's not milk'.

But he took it all the same and they both braced themselves for the rain, Gaughan in the transport box behind with Reilly's dog.

Reilly always kept a good tractor; he was aloof and insolated in the heated cab while Gaughan tried to hunch with the dog against the rain. Reilly drove into the night through the potholes and around the bends as if he had a bag of coal in the transport box. When he pulled into his yard, Gaughan gathered his groceries and limped towards his own place. They exchanged no words, Gaughan knew better.

The rain had dried off again and the moon was visible though a veil of high cloud. The drains were full and breaking out over the road in a wash of leaves and gravel. He could see the white wall of the front of his house as he sat down on a rock to draw his breath.

At this time of night women came into his head. He could have had a life like his brother in Coventry, three kids and a woman who looked after him. Could he have worked on the car assembly line for two week's holidays in Brighton? he pondered. He was groomed for the land and came home after his father died.

He lit a Major and looked up at his house. He thought of Betty. He couldn't comprehend her getting old and the boy, he imagined him at the school with that Mrs McCarthy she often said he liked, but now he was in his twenties. He got up before he sank into thinking about them.

The moon now had focused and the houses in the valley were illuminated. He knew them all too well, he thought to himself and what they were doing now. Mary O'Dowd propped up in bed reading her favourite book, *Orchids in Victorian Society* by TC Lyons as her husband waited, then finally gave up and fell asleep; Johnny Farrell, his ear to the radio, listening to the sea area forecast from the BBC; Mrs Kirby whispering prayers to herself in a cocoon of Foxford blankets for her only son in Chicago; Old Healy draining the last of a Power's whiskey bottle as he spits in the fire; the priest in a huge double bed shivering alone. He knew them and couldn't envy any of them, only their ability to continue. He wondered did any of them ask why, what was this absurd picnic about? He pushed in the door and stripped off his clothes onto the floor before falling into bed.

Gaughan woke up early the following morning. The moon was drifting down towards the ocean before the sun killed it off. He drank four china cups of water from the tap before he looked out. Already the wind was picking up and low clouds were spreading from the south, scudding along the horizon to the west in long streaks. He looked at himself in the mirror, felt his chin and decided he'd get away without shaving. A bucket rattled along the concrete yard, the dog was barking in the hayshed.

He went back to bed and put on the radio. The weather forecast issued a gale warning – 'south west winds would reach gale force on all coasts of Ireland and the Irish Sea and reach strong gale force from Valentia to Erris Head to Fair Head, frost in the eastern half of the country would clear quickly as a warm front approached from the west'.

Gaughan turned over in the bed and slept until the Angelus bell woke him.

He opened the curtains. The trees and bushes were being whipped by the gale, plastic bags were trapped in a corner of the garden and the first drops were cutting into the puddle of water in the yard which he used as a gauge to measure the type and intensity of the imminent downpour. He set the fire in the range before filling himself a bowl of cornflakes. He'd have to check the sheep before the rain got too heavy.

Down the valley, smoke from the cottages was being sucked away to the north-east. His was the last house without a fire. The dog greeted him at the back door and he dumped some potato skins he had on the table into a bucket with sour milk. The black coat he pulled on was heavy with dampness, it never dried properly but it was adequate with a cap to shelter him from the light rain.

The sheep were gathered in a bunch at the bottom of the field looking into a deep drain, being pushed into it by the gale. He drove them away up the field under a hedge but they returned, pushed back by the gale, to gaze in a dumb stupor at their own reflections in the bog water. When he got back to the house the postman had come and gone but still nothing, only a bill from the Co-op for barbed wire and another for the TV license.

He decided to have the dinner before he went into the village. In the shed he pulled out carrots, potatoes and a turnip from behind the parked tractor, the battery taken out where he tried to recharge it. The rain was heavier now and drumming on the galvanized roof in waves. As he scrubbed the carrots he looked down the valley. Already the day was over, he thought. He turned on the radio.

'Joe', said the lady on *Liveline*. 'Joe, the Corpo won't take our rubbish anymore'.

'And why?' asked Joe.

'Because we refuse to pay'.

'That's a disgrace', said Joe, 'I can't believe that they won't take it. I can't believe it'.

'It's a public health hazard', said the lady.

Gaughan cranked the dial to off.

Gaughan had eaten the dinner when he remembered he had to make another phone call to the headage office. He put on the oilskins over the damp coat and went down to Reilly for a lift.

'Come in, come in', Reilly wasn't long out of bed, was carving up a cold piece of bacon and cutting the hard butter into slices to place it on white bread.

'The kettle is on'.

'When will this weather clear?' asked Gaughan.

'When it starts in November it's often Paddy's Day before you get a spell. Then it gets hard from the east and you can set the mountain on fire to clear the old grass'.

'I know that', said Gaughan. 'What's the forecast for the week?'

'Even the cat knows that it's rain spreading from the west', said Reilly. 'I haven't all the spuds dug yet, they'll rot if I don't get them out soon'.

Gaughan lit up a Major.

'I need to ring Castlebar again today before they close. Will you drop me down when you're going?'

Reilly scraped a wedge of fatty bacon into a bowl for the dog, mixed it with dog food and presented it to the dog in his shed. He loaded two bales of hay neatly on the transport box and revved up the Ford as he went down the road with Gaughan. The dog running after them barked as he pulled in at a gap, cut the bales open and dumped them into half a ring feeder at the side of the road. The six cows plunged their heads between the bars as they sunk into the mud around the feeder, the suction associated with movement anchoring them to the same spot until the hay was consumed after which they would chew the cud oblivious in the rain for hours, their teats dipped in the churned mud. Eventually one by one they would retreat for shelter into the whins and lie there until the next visit by Reilly the following day.

When they pulled into the village Gaughan got a column of fifty pences from the barman and went straight to the phone.

'Thank you for calling', the voice said and it went on, 'press 3 for ...'

He fed more coins in from the column of fifty pences he placed on the windowsill but it just kept spitting out language. Then to Gaughan's surprise a woman answered.

'Don't leave down the phone', Gaughan begged. 'Do you know anything about the headage?'

'They're all gone home', she said. 'The offices close at three. I'm only the cleaner. You need to talk to Patricia or Bernadette. Bernadette deals with surnames from a-h but she's on a half day tomorrow'.

'I'm very grateful to you for answering the phone', Gaughan was trying to sound not too angry.

'Ring again tomorrow', said the lady and the phone went dead.

Gaughan was grateful that there was a human being there. He lowered a pint in two gulps and bought one for Reilly. The barman turned on the country music channel for McGuire. Dolly Parton was singing *Jolene*.

'It's direct from Nashville', said McGuire, 'direct'.

'I don't care if it's direct from Hiroshima, it's still shit', said Gaughan.

'Dolly can sing as good as anyone'.

'Look McGuire, Dolly sounds better with the volume down, all picture, no sound, that's the Dolly we all love'.

The barman was getting annoyed.

'It's back to CNN if ye don't stop'

'Any news on this fucking weather?' asked Gaughan.

'There's a half day promised dry next Tuesday', answered Reilly.

'That's a week away, which half?'

'The morning', Reilly replied.

The afternoon light had faded when the NCF van arrived. Ward concentrated on the order for milk and meats while the driver flung a string of stale sausages at the village dogs.

'We have a new type of butter out now', said the driver 'to add to our list of innovations. It's called Connacht Spread made from pure Connacht milk', said the driver winking at Ward.

'Does it spread? The butter's like a stone', said Ward.

'It spreads like shit from a cow on after grass'.

'I'll take it so', said Ward.

The small woman came in on Thursday nights with her husband Jackson, the man with the big tractors who owned around two thousand sheep. Everyone listened to him, he didn't say much. He knew the crowd in the headage office and was in Castlebar that day. Sometimes he'd buy drink for everyone after the mart. He always carried at least a grand in cash but drove a wreck of a pickup. Sometimes his wife would talk in a low voice and everyone had to be silent. She always knew when the cheques were due and she seemed to say they were out.

After an uncomfortable silence, Quinn blurted out.

'The price of sheep never goes up until after Ramadan'.

'When is that?' asked McGuire.

'It's like our Lent here, but it starts in the back-end'.

'It was Charlie Haughey who put a floor under the sheep, he could talk to the Arabs', said Ward.

'Takes one to know one', said McGuire.

'Didn't he drain the bogs', said Ward.

'It was the Board of Works', said Quinn, 'they do it every ten years'.

'The bank machine can't work in the new bogs, the hopper is the only job', said McGuire.

'There's men in this parish who get free coal and them sitting in the bog and they're not too far from you', McGuire went on. 'I know them and you know them and there's another man who gets an allowance for feeding the dog. Didn't I send the dog out the last day after the cows and on my solemn oath but didn't he get stuck in the muck and I had to send the children to pull him out'.

McGuire looked up to see was anyone laughing.

Gaughan and Reilly had lost the talk at this stage, they wavered slightly back and forward and agreed with everybody. The bachelors were as yet stoical and hadn't condescended to speech. Outside everything had changed, the wind moderated to a fresh north-westerly, the rain ceased and the moon was reflecting off hayshed roofs.

Reilly gave Gaughan a lift at closing time as before and Gaughan stumbled home. He sat on the rock again looking for answers, smoking a Major. He hoped he'd fall asleep before the drink wore off. The moon was almost full; it reflected sharply off the white walls of the cottages, his one the only one without a light. He could see Reilly's light go off after he fed the dog as the valley settled down for the night. His house was the last on the road.

He pulled the farm gate after him and tied it with barbed wire to keep the sheep out. As he approached his house he could see the branches waving, throwing shadows across the garden. He walked between the trees, turning the hardened reality of his life over in his head. He sucked his cigarette until it quenched at the filter. Why did he leave Coventry? Where was she now? And the boy. Maybe she sent him to university? Maybe the brother would find him.

He pushed in the door. In the house, shadows everywhere leaving sharp images. He wanted to feel the old people now. He didn't turn on the lights as he moved around the house, listening, their presence everywhere, faded photos catching the light, family celebrations, when his sister married, his parents' fortieth wedding anniversary, the time the Yanks came home and took pictures of everyone, all dead now.

The house, reeking with absence, was too much. He wanted them to give him a clue. If they were here now they'd have some answers. How could his life have thickened without warning? He opened a bottle of Powers whiskey and turned on the radio. It was Ralph McTell singing *The Streets of London*. He sang along to the chorus as it deepened his melancholy.

The old people seemed to be swimming through the walls and it soothed him as the shadows from the branches washed across his face. He got up and went into their bedroom which he hadn't opened for years. Nothing was changed since the day his mother was carried out of the room. He collapsed in her armchair as tears developed.

The window was open and there was a box of cattle tags, too big to go through the letterbox. The headage cheque landed on the carpet. He looked at them but couldn't get up. From where he was now, it didn't matter. Nothing mattered.

My Big Day

It was late November. The land was saturated from continuous rain and storm for weeks but that day was calm with a low cloud lurking on the horizon to the east. I was looking forward to Christmas breaking the monotony of winter. We were building a wall in the village on the Scheme, well it's called 'Working Together as a Team for a Brighter Future', but nobody can remember that. We're supposed to know that if the boss calls and we have to wear these stupid yellow jackets too. Keane and me were nearly finished for the day when a black fog blew over us and quenched the sun. Suddenly it was dark and the street lights came on.

We had cleaned the cement mixer, washed the shovels and had just locked the hut when we heard a strange noise coming through the fog from the east. Then came the funeral bell. What was happening, I thought – a funeral bell at four o'clock in the day? Keane looked frightened. It was our job to put traffic cones outside the church for weddings and funerals. Sometimes it's hard to tell the difference, Keane laughs at that, but I think there is some truth in it.

The noise became louder as if an army was marching and we heard a low drumbeat. Then we saw this form emerging, a white coffin and six men carrying it. Behind them ten others all in black and the drummer at the rear all heading for the church. At the end of the cortege a woman concealed in a wedding dress and veil walked out of step with the others. Another strange thing too was that the coffin seemed to be empty. I knew by the way they were carrying it. It was as if they were looking for a body. We had been mixing concrete on the road and it was in need of sweeping.

'It'll be alright', said Keane, but I started sweeping it to show respect. I had it all cleaned and then I threw a few buckets of water over it. They waited until I was finished and when they passed the lady looked into me and dispensed a tight, perfect smile. I felt as if something was leaving me and I would receive a small cold gift in return.

Soon they reached the church where the priest was waiting. I pitied the priest that day, he had to say Mass at nine that morning for the first Friday – even though there was only three there – then at ten he had a baptism, at twelve a wedding and now this funeral that came without notice. He looked flushed after coming home from the Royal Hotel. When the cortege stopped the lady walked casually to the front. The priest asked her the usual questions, who was her husband – he assumed it was her husband – what parish was the deceased from, what was his occupation and tell me, asked the priest, as he closed the hardback ledger, 'was he a family man?'

The woman was taller than the priest. She looked through him. Then she took a small silver axe from her black handbag and struck a blow at the church wall. The blood drained from the priest's face as if he knew what this meant. He waved them into the church where a few curious locals available to the priest at short notice had gathered at the other end. The prayers were said in Latin to which only the strangers responded. Keane and I stayed at the bottom of the church in our yellow jackets and I answered a few Latin responses from my time serving Mass with Fr Quinn. Again the woman looked over at me as if she always knew me, as if she was family. I felt something was happening to me and I couldn't stop it. When the priest left the church we waited outside for a smoke, to find out who these people were and what was their connection with the parish. Would they invite us for a half whiskey in McNamara's? The group in black assembled outside until the lady, radiant in her white dress, strolled to join them. Then they left in formation following her, walking out the road they entered, into the fog.

That night strange things happened. Cattle died and hay sheds went on fire. Neighbours blamed each other for their misfortune and started fighting in the pub. Old spleens almost forgotten came to the surface about rights of way in bogs. A tall woman dressed in black came to my house at midnight, told me about the fires and what was being said in the village.

'They say it's you that's behind it', she said. 'Do what has to be done', she pleaded as she walked away taking long strides in her flowing dress.

The priest was seen walking around the church. There was a fire in the graveyard. Nobody slept. At four in the morning the church bell tolled.

The next day I went to work with Keane as usual. He wouldn't talk and wouldn't look at me in the eye. Everything we did was useless, so much so that we knocked the wall we were building that evening. The dark fog persisted all day and it started freezing after the Angelus. Around four o'clock the bell tolled again and through the fog from the east came the strangers, this time the woman was in front taking long strides. She seemed determined, as if on a mission, her wedding dress flowing behind her. Keane had left the mixer beside the gravel out on the road. I ran down to pull it in out of her way in case she'd trip – new health and safety regulations, the boss is always on about it. She glared at me. She stopped. Her face changed suddenly. I felt a terrible shiver. Then she turned round and walked back east, slowly from the direction she came. The group kept going, entered the church, retrieved the coffin and left following her. As I walked back towards the church the fog lifted. All that was left was the faint sound of the drum.

When I looked out to the west the sun was out again, just like the previous day. Keane started talking as if nothing had happened, but that was when the trouble really started for me.

'Do you think we should order more cement?' I asked him. We had used almost a half ton since the previous day.

'No, there's plenty', he kept saying, denying that yesterday happened.

'Well there's only a bag left and we'll be idle unless we order more', I insisted. 'The gravel is running low too'.

'Looks the same pile to me', he insisted.

'Listen', I said, 'let's check the hut and we can count the bags'.

He seemed annoyed but I opened the lock.

'Look', I said, but there were eleven bags left.

'Now', he said, 'you're a day ahead of yourself. Maybe you could tell me more things about tomorrow?' he joked.

I didn't say much after that, just kept agreeing with him.

That evening I went to the village and talked about yesterday. I asked questions indirectly and referred to the fog.

'There was no fog out our way', or 'no fog back our side' was all I could hear. I met the people who were in the church that day but nobody would talk about it, insisting that it didn't happen and changing the subject as if I was embarrassing. There was only one answer for it and that was to go to the priest. I called up to get a Mass card signed for John Joe McGuire's mother. When I pressed the doorbell he answered immediately but he wouldn't let me in. After signing the card I referred to the fog but he denied that the black fog came. I complimented him on the Latin prayers but he smiled and closed the door.

I went home to turn this over in my head. What about the dead cattle in the haysheds? I drove around and sure enough the sheds were burnt and the cattle dead. I asked what happened.

'A terrible thunderstorm killed the cattle and struck hay sheds. Never saw the like of it', one man said.

'How can you have a thunderstorm and a calm foggy night at the same time?' I enquired.

'Around here it was storm and rain all night'. He was less than a mile from the village. At least yesterday happened, I thought, but nobody else would talk.

When I started talking to Keane the following day I suggested after a while that we'd go look at the church as it needed painting. The FÁS crowd are not supposed to be painting the church but the priest said he'd supply the paint and somehow we were told to do it. We have to paint the statues outside too. Keane asked the boss if we were painting the Protestant church too, but he got a strange vacant look and then we all laughed. I coaxed Keane to inspect the church at lunchtime.

'What about this mark?' I pointed to the track of the axe made by the woman.

'Jesus', he said 'Who done that? That needs to be painted over. And look where it is, right under the crucifix'.

The shape did not conform to that made by an axe but more like a letter from a strange alphabet.

'How did that happen?' I asked him.

'It must be after the disco, them young bucks can get up to anything'.

We agreed to approach the priest, who was thrilled to hear that we were going to start soon.

'Magnolia', he suggested. 'It's better than that light yellow that's on it'.

'What's the difference?' I asked.

'We need change, time now for a change, men'. He was firm about this. I knew not to challenge him

'There's one bit, Fr, that we need your advice on. Can we meet you around five o'clock after work?' I insisted.

He agreed. We'd meet under the crucifix.

'What class of a shape is that Fr, and what does it mean? You're an intelligent man', demanded Keane.

The priest developed a low voice. 'Paint it immediately, start here'. He frightened Keane.

'Yes Fr, we'll start in the morning', Keane reassured the priest as he walked away. There was something going on but I had learned not to ask questions.

We started painting and finished that wall before the day was out. There was great drying despite the time of year and the new rollers the priest got in the Co-op were fairly covering the rough pebbled dash. The magnolia was nearly like the old paint and we knew that we'd get away with the one coat.

'What are ye painting it again for?' Mrs Creighton scoffed. 'Isn't it fine, wasting money. Is that where our money goes on a Sunday?'

We had the church nearly finished in two weeks. There was only one wet day and a lively warm breeze blowing. The belfry was full of dead jackdaws but there was no point in talking to the priest about it. We offered to put up a net, but he wouldn't hear of it. We brought down the priest for his opinion. He just went straight to the spot.

'Why', he kept saying, 'did you miss that bit?'

He was pale with rage. Sure enough didn't the shape made by the axe come through the paint.

'We'll paint that again', said Keane. 'It needs an undercoat'.

The priest walked away.

'He's gone a bit odd lately', Keane commented. 'He's quit the golf, I hear and he's stopped giving sermons'.

As the weeks went by no trace of that day remained. The burnt sheds were rebuilt and filled with hay and turf. Nobody talked of what had happened and soon after the haysheds were completed the farmers denied that they were ever burnt down. Keane was looking forward to Paddy's Day, the Christmas having come and gone without event. It was my job to be St Patrick as part of the Scheme.

The parade usually starts after last Mass with St Patrick on the back of a Toyota pick-up, then there follows all the other vehicles owned by McNamara's garage. He got the Toyota agency last year after he built on a new showroom. Then there follows the tractors, usually the new ones first, owned by McNamara's brother who cuts the silage and puts out the slurry, and finally there's McNamara's brother-in-law who owns the shop, pub, petrol pumps, he's also an auctioneer and an undertaker. He usually drives by in his new hearse. At the end of the parade the children from the local National School are dressed in green and red, the county colours; they carry green balloons. They're practicing in the school yard for about a month before, except the Confirmation class who are studying Christian Doctrine for their big day.

The parade starts at the back door of the church and we drive around the village past the teacher's house and then Guard Burke's house, turn left at the bridge, past the old dispensary, down the hill to the lake where the grotto is decked with daffodils and back up again by the barracks, stop outside the front of the church and finish up in the pub where the cocktail sausages are sponsored by McNamara's. It's the first day since Christmas that some people are seen and the drinking can be serious.

It was dry, unusually warm and everyone was in high spirits. We followed the usual route until we came to the church. I was waving and blessing everyone for at least two hours, looking forward to a few pints at that stage when the pick-up cut out – Keane was driving it.

'Pull out the fucking choke', I ordered.

The funny thing was that we couldn't push it out of the way either. Then the bell started ringing but nobody was near it and when I looked up at the mark under the cross I noticed that it was back again even after being painted over several times. It took one of McNamara's new tractors to pull the little pick-up out of the way, leaving the road torn up and a smell of rubber. When we retired towards the pub I noticed that it was closed. Everyone seemed to know why, as they all filtered home, leaving me and the priest looking up at the mark on the church wall.

I was hoping now that the priest had realized that he had made a mistake. He paced around the church all day praying aloud as if looking for forgiveness. He shouldn't have painted over the mark again and again; he shouldn't have questioned the lady about the corpse, I thought. He shouldn't have told the farmers to rebuild their sheds as quickly as possible. He shouldn't have insisted that that day be wiped from the history of the village.

'Are you ok, Fr?' I asked.

'Everything is fine', he answered in that low voice. I knew now that to suggest that anything was wrong to him or to anyone in the village would be a mistake and could mean trouble. The wife or my kids could suffer.

'It's great to see the sunshine', I went on.

'It's great to see the sunshine, we seldom see it fine on Patrick's Day', he stated.

Soon after that day I noticed people stopped talking to me. They would say, 'a fine day, great growth', or 'there's a sting in the wind', but that was it. The wife and the kids started going a bit strange too. The pub would clear as soon as I entered. Maybe it was me that went strange. I tried hard to be normal but the more I tried the more they shunned me. If I challenged them they just said that there was nothing different and everything was fine.

After painting the mark unsuccessfully again the priest insisted that the whole wall be re-plastered but he wouldn't allow me near the job. It was as if the only connection left to that day was me and that famous mark. I lost my job shortly after that. Well the new boss interviewed me again and it seems that they were rolling out a new programme and that going forward I was not deemed to be adequately motivated as a team player. I felt now that whatever misfortune visited the people of the village that it was my fault.

I stayed in the house most days apart from looking after the sheep. Nobody ever called to see me. The summer and autumn passed by, I can't remember them really. The local doctor called out one day to the house. Herself met him at the gate. He said I had osteoporosis – trouble with the bones – sure enough the joints, especially the hip, was giving me bother. I took the tablets, she made sure I did.

Then one day I fell out on top of myself when I was dosing the sheep. That took the talk off me. The ambulance brought me away. It was during school-time so I didn't have a chance to say goodbye to Aoife and Sean. I lost track of time, whatever they did to me, but the funny thing was I didn't really miss anyone except the family. I seemed to be in good health, but they said I had a weak heart. I wasn't sure what I was doing in this place, they all seemed to be fairly healthy.

I don't know where the time went but anyway the wife kept me tuned into the months. The November rains were driving into the huge draughty windows in the hospital when it dawned on me. I'd have to get out on the anniversary of that day. I asked the nurse to arrange it – I'd pay the taxi – but not to tell my wife and family. They gave me my money, enough for a meal, a few pints and a bed and breakfast.

It was around four in the afternoon when I passed through the village, the bell tolled and a fog came down as I passed the mark on the church. I noticed the plastered wall at the mark was darker than the rest of the wall and a trickle of blood came from the spot, the strange shape was coming through. Odd things happened again that night. The priest's house got burnt down and Keane's heifer got drowned in the river. Three of McNamara's new Toyota Corollas went on fire too. They brought me back the following day around four and the fog seemed to lift as I was leaving.

Years passed, how many I'll never know, my wife and children stopped visiting me and life was different. They had me working in the garden where I was in charge of the lettuce and onions but nobody ate these anymore. I took up handball again. The only person willing to play was an old woman from Ballyhaunis who eventually just sat down in the nettles at the back of the alley. I was reduced to playing my right hand against my left hand. I always gave the left ten aces over the right and the old woman smoking a Sweet Afton kept count. I lost my position in the garden – well, they put me in charge of radishes, but I knew that this was demotion. I insisted that I was a team player and the man in charge of the gardens assured me that my contribution was gratefully acknowledged and that we were all working together as a team for a brighter future going forward.

I always got a calendar each year so that I didn't miss my annual visit home. The shop and pub had closed down, even the church had windows broken in it. Nettles were growing out through the school windows.

One year, I think it was this century, the taxi man dropped me out in the morning. He had to collect a football team in Swinford – it was the finals of the under sixteens – and he'd collect me at the church again, 'at six sharp'. It was a foggy day as usual and I enjoyed wandering in the village and around the family home. There were holes in the roof and weeds growing in the bedrooms. The graveyard seemed to be full of people I knew. Even some of the children who passed me on the way to school while I was working on the Scheme were buried there.

I decided to go into the church. I was shocked to find a coffin there, a large white one, just like the one that was carried into the village on that day, except that there was no lid on it. It was then that I heard the bell at four o'clock. I watched as the back door opened and they arrived as before, followed by the lady in the wedding dress. She walked up to me. The priest suddenly appeared from nowhere.

'Don't you accept that you are mine?' she proclaimed.

'I do', I said.

She smiled that tight, perfect smile. It seemed like what I was supposed to say. Then I stepped into the coffin. It felt nice sitting up in it as I was carried down the church which was now packed with friends and family. Outside, the whole village was throwing confetti at us as we were driven round the village in McNamara's hearse. The priest was smiling, pointing to the place on the wall where the mark had been. Then the hearse stopped exactly where I first met her when I was on the Scheme and the six men dressed in black lifted me out and carried me shoulder high in the open coffin. She walked triumphantly behind in her long flowing wedding dress as we headed east. The fog enveloped us as a single drumbeat announced my final departure.

Seventeen and a Half Minutes

It seemed like a normal morning with a touch of mist and fog when Nigel set off walking for school. He would get a lift when he got to the main road into town. He was just past the bridge when he noticed a red-faced man approaching him on a bicycle. He jumped of the bicycle and grabbed the boy by the lapels.

'You little fucker ya! Who asked you to come over here from London? That's our place. When that old woman dies we'll knock the wall from our field. Put up a new gate the next day. We're grazing it now for fifteen years'.

His eyes were red, water running from them.

'The McHales will control all the land around here soon so fuck off back to where ya came from, ya Cockney ponce'.

He dropped Nigel in a drain and cycled across the bridge into the fog. Nigel got up, cleaned the mud off himself and ran towards the main road, anxious that he wouldn't miss his lift from Mrs Grimes.

His mother moved to the country after his father went back to England. She couldn't afford to live on her own so she moved in with the boy's grandmother in her old house. There was no work in Mayo and his father was glad to be back driving a tower crane. She was lost living among wild farmers who couldn't understand her East London accent. Nigel didn't like the country and was always cycling back into the town. He liked the neat houses down near the sea, the gardens and especially the beech trees they had preserved when building. He dawdled beside the quays, the old boats and the little beach where he used to walk his dog before his parents separated. Cycling past his old house he strained his neck to see what changes were being made, to look at the oaks he planted there. He visited Mr Steward's shop where he worked last summer for three weeks in his new nursery potting out shrubs in the polythene tunnel. Then he cycled through all the streets in the town along the river bank before heading out past the quarry into the bog between the low hills and finally to his grandmother's place overlooking the bleak slopes of the mountain.

The town lads had become superior since he left and disowned him, especially the middle class ones living on the coast road. Some of the boys he played with were in boarding schools while others were polite but distant as if he had betrayed them. Their mothers never invited him to birthday parties since he left. His girlfriend too seemed to classify him as a loser, never available to go for walks with the dog on the beach. She never inquired where he was living, just referring to it as 'your new house in the bog'. Sometimes it seemed to him that he had learned a lot about his neighbours and friends and was learning about himself too. He didn't belong anywhere anymore. He would never belong again.

As he cycled past the bogs and the occasional holly or rowan tree he began to like the idea of not being attached to anything. The deadening loyalty to a place was not for him. In some ways he was grateful for his exclusion. He would never be a shopkeeper's son or a farmer's son, their futures laid out before them. His future would be full of adventure, he thought, as he cycled harder up the hills to his grandmother's old two-storey house. In the country the village lads mimicked his accent as they drove huge tractors to collect diesel and sheep nuts in the local Co-op. His mother had grafted her accent onto him. His father had lost his Irish accent as soon as he left the village at sixteen.

He had loved the heat in London; the trips with his mother to Brighton or the Tate Gallery on Sundays. The family moved back to Ireland when Nigel was sixteen, giving him two years to study for the Leaving Cert. His other grandmother lived in a house on the Old Kent Road. Nigel spent all his summer holidays there. Mr Foster offered him a job in his nursery. His father had gone back to Ireland then, building the house they would eventually sell after they separated. He often went into the city with his friends to buy a Rolling Stones t-shirt or a Jethro Tull LP. Nigel was a curious boy, always looking up at birds or catching insects. He liked to paint and his English art teacher had always said that he should be sent to art college. His Irish grandmother wanted him to work in the Co-op for the summer.

'It will make a man out of him', she said.

He was good with the books and knew exactly what stock was in the yard when he worked there at weekends. The manager kept him in the office and left the country lads driving the fork lift and throwing bags of feed into the car boots of the big Fords the farmers always bought.

In school Nigel excelled at English and Art, but made little progress with Irish or Chemistry. The teacher from the Gaeltacht – Ó Catháin – took a particular interest in Nigel, not only in his Irish but also in his Gaelic football skills, determined to kill his interest in soccer, anxious that the boy would not hold up the rest of the class. The left-handed pupils, and those who stuttered, were brought up to the front of the class together with Nigel. Ó Catháin would walk around the room, slowly beating the leather off the corners of the seats.

'Now men, I want to make myself clear, perfectly clear. If you fail Irish in the Leaving Cert you fail the Leaving Cert and there's only one place for you then. What's that?'

He hit the leather off Gallagher's desk.

'The boat sir'.

'Correct, *an báidín* boys. Now nobody, repeat nobody, will be failing Irish for the Leaving Cert. You may have had difficulty in the Inter Cert with Mr Burke but with me there won't be any. The class will be conducted in Irish next year. We'll all be singing like canaries *as Gaeilge* after you stay in the Gaeltacht for the summer. What will we be singing like, Nigel?'

'Like canaries', Nigel replied in his cockney accent.

Wednesday afternoons were reserved for sports, which meant Gaelic football or being confined to the school library. Ó Catháin excelled in the winter afternoons. They togged out under bushes and whins. The new dressing rooms were closed and kept clean for the senior GAA team. The pitch was fairly level except for the swampy areas near the goal mouth and another area where a drain was blocked; seagulls landed there occasionally. Ó Catháin was always well wrapped up, racing up and down the pitch, ready to penalize any minor infringement with vigorous blowing of the whistle. Sometimes a fragile, leggy boy would get shouldered into the puddles, coming out dripping mud and shivering between the showers of hail. The big leather ball flying through the air, smeared in mud, with the lacer spinning out of it, whipped against faces. It was impossible to kick far on account of its dead weight. Nigel was always put in goal. Sometimes the wind blew away from his goal and both teams, unable to kick against the gale, were confined around the far goal. At half time they were changed around and Nigel was then in the firing line. He was useless, hating the brutality and the fights that would break out, which Ó Catháin seemed to ignore.

'Hit him, he's no relation', they'd say.

He remembered the cricket grounds in London sometimes, when the sky cleared in early summer and the smell of lawns wafted down onto the pitch.

It wasn't unusual for Nigel to be beaten for missing a spelling or not pronouncing words according to Ó Catháin's rigorous standards. Sometimes he'd develop a stutter when answering the teacher, as the teacher walked around the room lashing the empty desks with the leather.

'Take it slowly now, Nigel, but get it right for a change', he would say.

Nigel seldom got it right and Ó Catháin would cut loose.

Since he left the town nobody had any sympathy for him. The town boys called him a bogger and the country boys called him a ponce. Nigel never liked the double Irish class on a Monday evening. When that was over he could feel the reprieve until the next Monday or the holidays.

The previous year it rained all summer and the farmers were unable to make hay and only retrieved poor, mouldy silage. There was no break in the rain and storm that autumn, resulting in cattle being hunted into sheds in September. After Christmas, farmers were anxious for an early spring. The rains finally stopped around the end of February, only to be replaced by winds from the Baltic. Soon the churned-up fields dried out, the grass went grey and withered down to the clay. Farmers bought hay and straw in the south until it ran out.

That March the Co-op manager approached Nigel to work on Saturdays. The Co-op couldn't deal with the demand for sheep nuts, dairy nuts and coal. The manager also asked him to find a mate in his class to help load the bags for the farmers. The boy liked the power of choosing one of his classmates. His remaining friends still belonged in the town or at least the ones he had anything in common with, but he needed someone who could haul coal and throw hundred-weight bags around like bags of sugar. He also needed an ally against bullies. He chose McHale whom he never talked to but he knew the manager would be impressed. He wanted to get on the right side of the McHale clan, the best he could hope for was that they would ignore him.

McHale's eyes lit up when he approached him in the school yard.

'No problem you ponce', he said, forgetting not to insult him. 'I mean Nigel', he threw back at him when he was long gone. It was McHale's dream job meeting the neighbours and maybe getting a chance to drive the fork lift.

'Where did you get that gorilla?' the manager asked.

'He's not afraid of work', Nigel said.

'He'll do, I suppose. We didn't hire him to do any paper work I hope. Keep him out of the office'.

McHale replaced the forklift with his own tractor when it broke down and the manager thanked Nigel with a few extra pounds which he shared with McHale.

'Thanks, ponce', he'd say forgetfully.

The spring didn't arrive until May. Nigel and McHale had a curious friendship built up. Nigel looked out for McHale in the Co-op, making sure he got overtime on weekday evenings when the Co-op opened late in the fodder emergency. McHale even began to call him Nigel and wouldn't let anyone touch him in the school yard or on the football pitch. Nigel knew this deal wouldn't last after the Co-op resumed normal hours, but McHale was a creature of loyalties and any assault on a friend of his was an attack on him.

Nigel was dreading the Monday after the Leaving Cert mocks. Ó Catháin had corrected the tests and Nigel didn't answer the grammar questions.

'No Irish grammar answers I see', he shouted at Nigel as he cowered in his seat.

'Did you ever hear of the *Tuiseal Ginideach*?' he shouted.

'Yes sir!' he pleaded. The boy's heart raced as he began to stutter.

'Up here', he demanded. Ó Catháin whipped ten belts of the leather across both hands. As the boy retreated Ó Cáthain shouted 'I'm only starting boy!' as he rolled up his sleeves. He slapped him across the face and said something about his mother. The boy tried to run away but the door was locked. Ó Cáthain, purple with rage, trapped him against a desk.

'What am I doing here with a fucking Cockney ponce trying to drill Irish into your thick skull', and broke into some tirade in Irish. The room was silent suddenly as Ó Cáthain reached for the leather again in an attempt to regularise the beating.

A voice from the back said, 'that's enough now'.

Ó Cáthain continued. He didn't appear to hear the low voice coming it seemed from another world. It was heard again by the class. It sounded like that of an old man, and this time Ó Cáthain also heard it. He raised his head as if it was coming from outside or maybe inside his head. He applied himself again and as he held out the boy's hand the words were heard in the same slow dead voice.

'I said that's enough'.

He lifted his head away from the boy and demanded to know whose voice it was.

'It's me. McHale. And I said that's enough now'.

'What would you know, you fucking bogman. Sure you wouldn't know your own ass on the road'.

He dismissed the boy and called up McHale.

'I'm here if you want to meet me', McHale said, not changing the dead tone of his voice.

Ó Cáthain, purple with rage, demanded his hand for the leather. McHale gladly obliged. Ó Cáthain jumped off the floor to gain the maximum impact, but McHale's hand tightened on the leather and he chucked it so that the teacher landed on top of him. McHale looked at him in the eye and said it again.

'I don't like to have to repeat myself, but I'll say it once more. That's enough now'.

The teacher was flailing at McHale, who at this stage was holding the teacher at arm's length. The class watched. McHale seemed irritated by the teacher who didn't seem to understand what was happening.

McHale had been approached by the Co-op manager the previous Saturday on Nigel's recommendation and was asked to stay on permanently, but he had decided to punch in his last week at school. McHale could see his life mapped out before him now. His ambitions to work on the forklift eventually would be realized, but for now he was stuck in this place for only a few more days. In some strange way he felt like an adult now, would have his own income soon, he would have a car, a girl and would start building his own house beside his father's on the family farm.

This had all happened in McHale's head since he was offered the job and now here he was with the *Tuiseal Ginideach* causing misery in his last school days. He wondered what all these five years in the Brothers were about. He loved welding and fixing farm machinery. That was all he wanted to do. He remembered the beatings he suffered from Ó Cáthain, the insults, the sarcasm, the jibes about his father, the 'Gorilla' name Ó Cáthain had given him. This all exploded in his head now. He knew when he went out working that Ó Cáthain would ignore him and he would never get the chance again. He enjoyed the spin on the school bus every morning, but he had no talk to charm the girls.

McHale lifted the teacher off the ground and placed him back in his chair, saying, 'that's enough now, don't ever touch my good friend Nigel again', but the teacher grabbed the cane and whipped McHale on the back of the head as he returned to his seat. McHale felt a trickle behind his ear.

'Open your books at page twenty seven', Ó Cáthain said, trying to sound normal.

McHale didn't open his book at page twenty seven. McHale never opened another book. McHale felt the blood trickle on the back of his neck and as he rubbed it and saw the colour of it on his hands and smelled it, something changed. He felt his muscles tighten as if his being was threatened. He grabbed the teacher by the jacket as tears of rage fell from his cheeks and then let him go. Ó Cáthain saw this as a weakness and decided to break him.

'Come on, McHale, we'll play it your way. Lock the door, Cockney ponce', he threw at Nigel, but Nigel was afraid to move. 'Lock the door', he shouted.

McGuire jumped up and locked the door. Ó Cáthain, fancying himself since he was a light-weight boxer in his home village of Rosmuc, got up and resumed a boxer's pose just to let the class know that he could wear down McHale with time and intelligent boxing skills. McHale didn't rise to the boxing as he grabbed the teacher and threw him against the blackboard. McHale moved slowly like some kind of primate with imminent plodding movements. The class became afraid of McHale now. This was a different place. Would McHale know when to stop? They knew the whole class would suffer somehow. McHale's friends beckoned to him, knowing now that he was out of control. He couldn't see anything, his eyes were dead in his head, focusing on Ó Cáthain as he tossed the teacher around like a scarecrow.

Then it happened. 'That's enough now' was heard again, but McHale, in the fever of open assault, could hear nothing. Again it was heard, louder. McHale could hear it now. He looked around to see fear on the faces of his classmates, his friends. This fear he knew. He looked at Nigel, dishevelled, pursing his lips saying something, but he couldn't hear it, the blood pumping around his body, his heart beating in his ears. It was coming from Nigel. He looked back to see Nigel again repeating the phrase as he nodded his head slowly. McHale obediently withdrew, leaving Ó Cáthain battered under the blackboard.

'Nigel, if you say that's enough, that's good enough for me', McHale said in a low voice as he plodded back to his seat.

They all waited for the bell to go, but there were seventeen and a half minutes left in the class. The teacher gathered himself and sat at his table.

Outside the rain was settling down for the day as it saturated the glass of the prefab, at first obscuring the view and then forming a shiny transparent film making it easy to see out through the dreamy distortions. Nigel could see the gulls swooping in the playground as if they knew lunchtime was approaching; the remains of white bread sandwiches would be there after the ham and cheese were eaten. The Protestant children from 2B were already feeding the gulls as they didn't have to attend Christian Doctrine class. The weeds were flattened in the relentless wind, thistles grew from cracks in the old mass concrete walls and ragwort bloomed where the prefabs were settled on blocks, suspended over perished tarmacadam.

Nigel looked up at the clock again for some reason, the minutes dragged in the gloom. Still sobbing, his glasses couldn't be found, his hair dishevelled, stains of tears on his cheeks, standing still. The rest of the class kept their heads down not daring to turn a page. The teacher pretended to be working in some ludicrous manner as if nothing had happened. There was a pool of piss under Nigel's left foot. Nigel finally remembered to sit down.

Something happened in those strange seventeen and a half minutes to everybody in that room. They would carry it for the rest of their lives. Nigel sat shivering in his wet clothes, his broken glasses had landed oddly on the ledge of the blackboard. Next door they could hear Brother Murphy leading the class through *Tantum Ergo* in preparation for the end of term mass.

Nigel wondered about his mother now, he felt something would happen to her. The ruddy face of the other McHale who had assaulted him at the bridge going to school came into his mind and he knew now that he was right. He would have to bring his mother back to London. He knew nothing would ever be the same again and wanted to run home and comfort her. The times he had spent with his father walking along the Serpentine in London before they came home seemed like a dream now as the waves of rain spread relentlessly across the school yard and out over the football pitch.

McHale too wondered what his new life would bring and waited for the bell to release him finally. He thought of the new tractor his father was going to buy to cut silage around the parish that summer, the Co-op and if all the fertiliser would be delivered that was ordered, and the forklift the way it could be steered with a finger on the knob of the wheel.

Nigel looked around the room at the cowering faces, at the large picture of Edmund Ignatius Rice, founder of the Christian Brothers. He took everything in now as if he knew these few minutes would change all of their lives. The tap dripped into the sink behind them, each drop startled. Nigel looked again at the clock, the hands had barely moved. He could smell his clothes as they dried into him. Nobody coughed, nobody moved. The *Tantum Ergo* came through the walls for another seventeen and a half minutes.

Jobs for a Wet Day

Reilly was on his second bottle of red Merlot after he got home from the karaoke in the Poachers Inn when the thought came to him. Why would he spend the whole day travelling to Galway waiting in the hospital when he could do the job himself? What was it only a fancy angle grinder used by an over-paid doctor to crack the cast open. This cheered him up but he decided to wait until the following day when he was sober. He looked at the broken arm for a long time as if it wasn't his, something alien that was adding to the catalogue of failure and old age creeping up on him. He couldn't meet her with the cast on. Would they let him on the plane? He wasn't sure if he could wait much longer, he had the ticket booked for the following Monday.

Already the dawn was lurking in the north-eastern sky which never darkened fully at the end of June. Soon the sun would be squinting behind the mountains and the crows heading south from the huge trees around the ruins of the church. He had seen too many dawns in recent years. He would turn over his memories and draw the same conclusions as he had done a decade previously, but now at fifty-four he wondered how it had come to this. He was tired now of pulling in on the way home from the Poachers and the Roma takeaway, eating the cod every Saturday night – the same shape as the melodica he played for Mrs Delaney in national school – and pressing the chips between his lips as he rounded the last corners before he abandoned the Defender in the hayshed.

Inez Martinez – he kept sampling the name as if it was some exotic liquor, turning it around in his mouth. He had met her in Galway the previous summer at a salsa party. She moved easily between the practiced moves he had been honing on the local girls at the winter classes in the vocational school – the machinery repair ones were cancelled. She sent him a card with her address from Guanajuato – you come to my city, Señor Reilly. He went.

One Monday morning instead of going to the mart as he had done for the previous twenty-four years he drove past the usual line of trucks and trailers and sped straight to Galway Airport, took the Aer Arann to London, then off on the jumbo to Mexico City. He could see the lakes in Connemara as a safety belt sign came off. What would he normally be doing now, he thought, sitting at the mart talking to neighbours about the price of straw or maybe fencing down the land in the company of the sheepdog. The lady beside him turned on his map showing the jumbo heading for the tip of Greenland before veering over the St Laurence, down along the east coast of the USA before cruising out over the Gulf of Mexico.

'What brings you to Mexico?' she enquired.

'I'm meeting someone', he replied.

'Sounds very secretive', she smiled.

'It's a woman', he admitted.

'So you're in love', she smiled.

'Maybe I am', he ventured, 'and you?'

'A man. I met him in Cancun, holiday romance when I was with the girls. We're getting married next year. He's living in Oaxaca. I'm moving from Tullamore after Christmas, taking Spanish lessons in the local VEC. How's your Spanish', she asked?

'*Manos arriba* is all I know, from the westerns', he laughed.

'You'll be fine', she smiled, 'are you thinking of moving?'

'No', he was adamant, 'and she can't leave with the small child'.

'You might have to change your mind like me', she shook her head. 'Love is a dangerous thing'.

Reilly smiled back as they both resumed reading the in-flight magazine.

He fell asleep for what seemed like hours. When he felt the jumbo descending he looked out the window and saw the mountains near. Soon the jet banked and thousands of shacks hanging onto hillsides came into view. It straightened again and suddenly they were on the ground. The girl beside him helped him through customs and soon he was at a huge bus station where she pointed him to a bus that would bring him to the metro. She hugged him goodbye.

Reilly was on his own now among 20 million people. He offered 50 pesos to the driver and soon he was at the metro station terminal. He had the station where his hotel was circled on a map in his jacket but he knew that to be seen with the map would make him a target. Mixiuhca, it was called. A mariachi band struck up beside a bunch of women making tortillas, they poured, tossed and flipped them effortlessly as the band smiled at everybody. Reilly checked the map and jumped onto what he hoped was the right train. He was the tallest in the carriage and kept both hands in his pockets with the bags between his legs. A blind man was playing a bottle with a nail, a one-armed man playing a mouth organ. For a while, the train went above ground where Reilly could see lines of prostitutes at the traffic lights and boys standing on their heads when the lights turned red, then collecting coins before they went green. He pushed himself out at his station and waved a taxi. At his hotel there were grilles on the windows and the receptionist took his passport and led him down a dark corridor to a room with no window. There was a large gap under the door.

'*Buenas noches, Señor*', she threw at him as she presented him with the keys.

Reilly collapsed on the bed only to see a scorpion on the wall. He killed it and kicked it out under the door.

The following morning Reilly was on the bus to Guanajuato. He could see the snow-capped volcano they call Popocatepetl in the distance. He passed lines of traders before they drove up the hills along the patchwork of shacks scratched into the parched earth. Reilly could see what seemed like crowds of people at every little crossroads carrying crates of chickens or making tortillas. He fell asleep as the bus settled into the smooth surface of a new motorway.

It was evening when the bus dropped him off at a bus terminal in Guanajuato City where he took a local bus to the centre, full of children and men with burnt faces. The bus plunged into a tunnel and soon Reilly had to get off underground, where he walked up to the daylight on another street. It was still warm.

'I meet you on Plaza de la Paz', she said, 'at the basilica at 8'.

Reilly lumbered across Juarez, towards the basilica. He was early and stopped to get a tortilla and a beer. *Cerveza*, the girl corrected him.

At home now he thought it would be around one o'clock at night. The usual crew would be leaving the Rendezvous, Barrett with the dog running after the red tractor towards the hill, Gaughan in a pick-up towards the lake and McGuire walking the short distance past the old dance hall to the council houses. Reilly would be cycling home, wondering was there any options to this, kicking a crust of hailstones in the moonlight as he fumbled for the door keys, rolling her name in his mouth as he pulled the blankets over himself and fell into oblivion.

Here he was now, with his boots up on a suitcase, a glass of beer and waiting for his woman. The only reminder of home was the electric fence wire he tied onto the handle of the heavy brown suitcase to reinforce it. As the basilica bell sounded, she appeared. He hardly recognised her, taller than he remembered, long black hair, boots. She greeted him with open arms and a long hug.

'John Joe, you most welcome to my *pais*', she couldn't remember the word for country.

'*Buenas días*', he uttered from the phrase book he read on the jumbo.

She held his hand as she ordered two beers.

'You like our beer', she enquired, 'like your Guinness, no?'

It's cow piss, he said to himself, but smiled and said, '*buenos, señorita*'.

She laughed at his handful of phrasebook words. Nothing he could do or say would stop her from falling in love with him. She held his hand crossing the square and up the steep slopes to her apartment. Her mother Maria had put Paco to bed and she now retired after welcoming Reilly and setting out several dishes for herself and Inez.

At breakfast they all ate like a family, Paco shy, looking up at the tall, pale-skinned man before going to school with his grandmother. Inez, off work for the month, brought Reilly into the city where they went to see the mummies in the museum. She told him how the mineral soil and the dry atmosphere combined to preserve the bodies which were exhumed when their relatives couldn't afford the upkeep fees. After lunch they took the funicular to the Pipila monument. There they gazed over the city while Inez pointed out the other monuments and explained how the city came to be, as a result of the discovery of silver.

Some days they did very little. After Paco went to school they would stroll through the streets, stopping in her favourite cafes before sitting in the park. Other days they went on trips, including one to Teotihuacan, where Reilly sat on top of the Pyramid of the Moon, gazing down along the Avenue of the Dead with the Pyramid of the Sun to the left. She wondered why the moon and its sacrificial altar were at the centre of the wide avenue while the Pyramid of the Sun was dismissed to one side.

February was nearly over the day they went to Xochicalco, where Reilly took fright as an iguana trotted up to him. Inez laughed so loud it made him sad. She was totally uninhibited and happy. He thought of home and he knew that the cows would soon be calving and that his neighbour Quinn would not be able to handle the Charolais calves.

'What will become of us?' she kept asking as she led him to the bus stop.

'We'll see, I'll write or ring you. I'll be back next year, don't worry'.

They hugged before he took the bus out of the tunnel and back to Mexico city, where he stayed in a cheap hotel near Allende metro station.

Reilly couldn't sleep that night. He felt in some strange way that he left his family behind, as if he was leaving a home to go to another home. There would be nobody waiting for him when he stepped off the Aer Arann plane in Galway. He would put the key in the door same way he always did as if he'd just returned from the Rendezvous after a night's drinking. He got up and walked around the street. It led to the huge square they called the Zocalo. Here Reilly wandered, looking up at the National Palace and the Cathedral. He wanted to feel these moments, to remember and to savour them for when the conversation would lapse in the pub. He lingered over two shots of mezcal which he'd developed a taste for over the month.

Early morning he grabbed a taxi to the airport, took a last glimpse at the shacks on the burnt hills through the window of the jumbo before flying back again over the US and out over the Atlantic. Soon he was fumbling in his pockets for the keys, as the cows lowed in the shed and the hailstones gathered in a corner beside the door. She sent postcards every week and photographs. He wrote once a month. She couldn't travel with Paco and her mother. He was anchored to thirty acres of rushes.

Two hours had passed since he sat down thinking about her. The sun was up but the clouds were already tumbling in off the sea as the weather man predicted. Another wet summer in Ireland was too much after a winter of relentless gales and rain. Inez Martinez, he rolled the name again as an antidote to his despair. He didn't know it yet but every time he repeated the exotic name he was saying yes, louder and louder to her latest invitation. He limped back into the house as if he had made some decision but he couldn't contemplate what was happening as he drifted into sleep.

He woke around noon. The cast was driving him crazy with itch as he tried to reach the spot with the poker. Her name again in his head repeating itself like country songs he had danced to in the Temperance Hall – drop kick me Jesus through the goalposts of life, or my tears have wiped I love you from the blackboard of my heart. He lit the gas and set up a fry. The postman had come and gone leaving only a notice of a lawnmower sale in the Co-op. He found himself looking at the atlas. He could find Mexico City but the jumble of cities in the mountains beside each other with names that crisscrossed on the map frustrated him and he threw the atlas on the couch. He busied himself that day tidying the shed. It was a job that he postponed several times but he now found himself diligently sweeping the floor and neatly filling the shelves with paint tins and small tools. Fencing wire and posts stored in a corner, he would have room to park the tractor inside. He didn't know why he was doing this. It felt like he was getting ready for something. His father always said you need to have jobs for a wet day, keeps the head from going soft, jobs like painting or putting handles in spades and shovels, cleaning sheds or burning rubbish and bedding.

The following day he pulled a dry cow to the mart. This was the second year that she wouldn't keep. He dumped the cow in the pen and picked up his number. He would be waiting three hours before the sale so instead of killing the day as he usually did trying to find out trends in prices he parked up the car trailer and went up town. He bought the *Irish Times* and went into the best hotel, the Imperial, and ordered fillet steak. He wasn't sure why he was there but it felt good. The local solicitors, the bank manager and an eccentric Englishman dined there for years.

'Can I make a phone call?' he asked the receptionist.

'Of course', she replied in a refined accent.

'I'll put it through for you, to where?'

'The mart', he said apologetically.

He could hear the loudspeaker and the staff on the phone.

'Hello', a voice shouted in a demanding tone.

'When are the dry cows starting?' he shouted back thinking he couldn't be heard.

'There are only ten of them so we'll run them through in an hour after the heifers'.

'Thanks', he shouted back.

The music – Satie's *Lent Et Grave* – coming from the musty hotel speakers couldn't drown out his sharp words and the Englishman recoiled as he resumed chasing peas around a pork chop. The receptionist handled the phone with two fingers as if it needed to be replaced or at least washed.

He read the paper from cover to cover and everything seemed to be interesting. The hotel was empty again and the warm sunlight crept along the reception counter where the girl was looking away. She was new but as neighbours they knew each other. He admired her legs, heels and long hair. It was nice being alone with her and to imagine that she might be kind.

'Finished', she interrupted his daydream as she grabbed the plate. She looked away as he paid and made a fuss of giving him the change so that he was forced to concede it as a tip. 'Thanks', she mustered a plastic smile as she looked into a place that must have been his neck.

Tourist traffic was choking the town now as he drove in the opposite direction up the hill towards the mart. He knew this road so well but somehow now it was different. The trailers parked on both sides of the road, the hawkers pitched out against the traffic and everywhere the smell of cow dung which irritated him now for some reason. The harsh loudspeakers rumbling away and the half-silence after the auctioneer shouted 'sold', drowned out by the other sales ring at a different stage in the tired process. He parked between an empty cattle trailer and a calf dealer allowing the tow bar to guide him against the wall. As he left the car the calf dealer stood in his way, whacked a piece of plastic piping on the bonnet.

'I'll give you two for four hundred euro'.

It seemed a great bargain but even though he knew the dealer he just said thanks in a limp indifferent way. He had often bought calves off him but now all he wanted was to sell the cow and leave. He passed the hawkers with their rows of wrenches and gates, the sun glinting off them made them seem sad and pointless. He knew almost everyone at the sales ring but he decided to sit high up behind the buyers and observe.

When his number was about to come up he went quietly to the sellers' hut beside the auctioneer where the other farmers were. His number was 67 but at 66 the next animal to enter the ring was 66A then 66B and it continued. He was angry now as some cute whore thought he was going to sell his lorry load of cows before him and delay him half an hour. This was typical of the way people are treated here he thought. Before he would have just gone back to the sales ring and chatted to other farmers, now he was too angry.

'There's twenty one cows coming in now ahead of you. We won't be long. You might as well have a cup of tea', the auctioneer laughed down at him as he waved the timber hammer at a bid and the dealer pushed him to one side.

He went out to the canteen but there he began to see more than he wanted to, as if a veil had been lifted. He ordered.

'It's a fiver even', he was told.

A cracked mug of tea and a rasher sandwich was pounded on the formica table, which rocked from side to side.

'Try this', a small fat man thrust a Major cigarette box folded twice to act as a spacer to steady the leg of the table, his dirty coat thrown across the table, a scratch of cow dung across his neck.

'The bullocks are well down, sure everyone has them bought at this stage for the grass'.

The fat man churned the mug of tea with a desert spoon as he began to clear a plate of sausages and chips. Then another taller man sat at the same table invading his space.

'It's a great year for grass', he declared and the two men spoke at length on the implications of this on the trade at the back end. They ignored him after a while and left their cattle sticks dripping with hot shit at the end of the table. Soon after, a rush of men came through the door from the ring and his name was called out on the loud speaker. The cow sales were over and his cow was the last. He rushed out to the auctioneer but the sales ring was almost empty.

'We had an SOS out for you. Were ya having a three course dinner and a glass of red Bordeaux?'

He cranked up the sales pitch again and coaxed three buyers about to leave the ring back. There was only one bid and the auctioneer knocked the cow down to one of his cronies.

'Go on you good thing', he winked at the buyer.

'That's what she said last night', the buyer retorted. 'Go on now, like myself you're too old for all that. It's bad for the pacemaker, she says'.

The buyer slapped Reilly on the back.

'Is the right hind quarter blind?'

'She's for the factory', Reilly replied, 'one way ticket, that won't bother you'.

'I'll throw her back if I don't get luck money'.

Reilly gave him a tenner which was followed by another whack on the back.

'You're your father's son', the buyer laughed.

The auctioneer was being fed at a special table with the mart manager, his white coat trailing on the saw dust. At the counter there was a selection of sticks and plastic pipes where mugs of boiling tea and rasher sandwiches were loaded up at one end. There was no change left so everything was in multiples of five euros. A bunch of men flushed through another door accompanied by the sheep auctioneer. One of them slapped a plastic pipe on the counter, 'two half ones', he laughed.

'That's a grand cow you had', a man put his hand on his shoulder, 'why did you throw her away cheap. Your father would never do a thing like that, God rest him. Tell me was one of her tits blind?' he inquired as if he was concerned.

'She's sold now', he replied.

Inez Martinez, he kept saying to himself as if he was holding onto something. He left the mart not wanting to meet anyone, the loudspeaker still booming in the bullock ring hurried him. Normally he lingered, talking to his neighbours but something was changing. He stopped in the small shop but here too the polite pleasantries of Ms O'Donnell annoyed him. He looked at her knowing that she too would soon be dead. He had to leave before he'd confront her as to why she stayed here year after year without a holiday. He wanted to ask her what was it all for, but he left in a hurry. Then he saw O'Reilly pulling in for petrol with three ewes in the back of a trailer. O'Reilly was nearly 60. He couldn't talk to him either. He couldn't ask is there a drop of the Suffolk in those border Leisters or who did your shearing this year? He couldn't talk about the Connaught Semi-Final or the price of weanlings in the back end. He knew that if he didn't go home soon that he'd catch someone and ask 'do you know what's happening or what's all this about?' but he knew he had to suppress it.

Soon he was turning up the gravelled track towards his house when he remembered that he had forgotten the trailer. He knew that something was wrong now. He stood in the kitchen looking around him as if it was the first time he entered his own house. The long summer evening stretched out before him. He looked up at the postcards from Inez and the photograph of them together at the statue on the hill. His parents were glaring down at him. Sunlight was streaking across the kitchen onto the cold range, the weight of the silence was too much. He ran outside. No place now seemed safe, his mouth was dry. He went walking down the fields to clear his head, carrying a spade. He could see jobs that needed to be done and frantically attacked them, building walls that were scattered for years, opening blocked drains, lifting stones from the middle of the field. Clouds were rushing across the sun, the wind was gathering, blowing sudden gusts into the bushes beside him. In the fading light he could see his house in the distance. He didn't want to go there yet. He sat down thinking of Inez, her voice might settle him he hoped.

All around him he looked at the hills and farmhouses as if for the last time. It was dark now, he had nowhere to go except back to the house. Inside in the thickening gloom he poured himself a Powers whiskey and fell asleep. He woke up around two in the morning at the sound of a tractor going home from the pub, his heart was racing as he poured another Powers. He tried to ring Inez but he had no bars on the reception. He rang again from the top of the hill as the rain was beating off the sheds. He wanted to tell her that his life had stopped making sense, that somehow they would have to come to some arrangement. Going over to Mexico again would only make his life a misery at the thought of returning to this hellhole without her.

In Guanajato as a storm grumbled on the horizon, Inez looked at her mobile as she closed the patio door against the hot wind blowing in from the country. Soon she would be dressing Paco for bed, making his lunch for the morning. She would ring back her boyfriend in Ireland after her quesadilla, he often rings when he is drunk, she thought to herself. She would remind him that she loved him.

Reilly returned in despair to the shed, grabbed the angle grinder and brought it into the kitchen.

'I have to get out of here soon', he said aloud.

It whined perfectly as he held it against the cast. It cut a perfect line along the length of his arm. I'm going to get out of this prison. He cracked a hammer against the cast but it didn't open up along the saw cut. He started the saw again. He didn't care now. It was as if the pain in his head was far worse than what might happen to his arm. In some way he thought if he could feel something in his arm it might divert the pain away from his mind.

'This fucking tip', he kept shouting to himself, 'where every loser is sitting in the passenger seat of his own life as if nothing is happening. Yes Ms O'Donnell', he mimicked her, 'it's very mild for the time of year, will the rain ever stop or will we just have to offer it up for the next life, isn't that the way'. The saw was discharging fine dust against the cups on the sideboard. 'Yes John Joe', he mimicked O'Reilly, 'if you give them a dose now and dip them you can forget about them till Christmas day or only for the few bob in the post they'd be a waste of time'. He could feel something now, a trickling sensation where the saw was tearing at the gauze next to his skin. He threw the saw on the floor.

'O Jesus what have I done', he shouted, as the blood squirted across the floral wallpaper. He grabbed the mobile. There were no bars.

You Do Know Who I Am?

Sometimes I go to Sligo, sometimes Cork or Galway, depending on the mood. I flicked a coin one day and it said Sligo. I was out the door fairly rapid and on the road travelling light. I always stop in a small town on the way where I get served tea and a scone in an old family-run coffee shop. The older woman always overcharges me, while trying to figure out where I'm from and where I'm going. I always tell her the truth, about flicking the coin and all that, but she never seems to believe me. It's like she thinks I'm daft or something. She has all her family photographs on the walls. Then she asks me am I married, before she introduces me to her daughter. It's always the same routine. I make apologies and say I look forward to seeing them both in the spring.

'What we need', she says to her daughter, 'is a man around the house'.

In my presence, imagine. The daughter looks away embarrassed. I have been presented with her daughter who is recently going grey for the last twelve years.

Then she shows me into the old bar. Nothing has changed since it was closed in the sixties; the old poster for the Cassius Clay/Sonny Liston fight, the advertisement encouraging us to drink Double Diamond and the Guinness one with the little man carrying the horse, old tin boxes for loose biscuits and a packet of Omo washing powder on the otherwise empty shelves. The daughter has long blonde hair tied up in a bun which she lets loose as we walk through the bar. The mother suddenly disappears and the daughter gets in my way. I pay the bill and leave.

Soon I'm on the road again, taking the scenic route in no rush, the skylark in full song as I approach the coast. I'm guessing I'll be in Sligo by one o'clock, but it doesn't matter, four is ok too. As I pull in towards the sea an old man runs out in front of me.

'Did you see any cattle on the road?'

'Yes', I say, 'but I passed them three miles from here. Jump in', and we catch up with the wild bunch of Limousine bullocks heading into the town.

'They broke out of the shed, in all winter and they're gone mad', he proclaims.

We pass them at the speed limit and turn them around. Their nostrils flared, froth coming from their mouths. They walk back towards this huge derelict house and slink into a cobbled yard.

'When did it get burned down?' I ask.

'There's only one wing burned down', he insists. 'The brother done that but I wouldn't leave'.

I follow him as he asks me in for tea. We go up to the third floor over bare stairs where weeds have taken root at the edges. There's a big timber latch into a room. I sit at an old formica table against a mossy wall. There's a bed in the corner and a portable TV. I notice a contraption in another room.

'What's that?' I ask.

'I push the weights there every morning, lived in San Francisco for a long time. You gotta keep the body moving, the Yanks know all about this stuff. I had to come over here when the old man died to sort out the place. This was worse than Alcatraz. The old man, nobody could live with him so I got out after the Leaving Cert. The younger brother stayed and took the shit. Me, man, I was into Morrison, not the Belfast guy now, *Riders on the Storm*, get my drift? Yeah, me and Kerouac, I used to gun the Buick from Montana to the Bay, then down to Tijuana for the weekend. Beats Athleague on a Saturday night, get my drift? You gotta pump the iron too, diet is only part of the deal. Look here, I can do stuff these dopey young fellas around here can't touch'.

He gave me a ten minute display of bench pressing.

'Clears the head too, good for the fuse box, man. You don't want a fire in the wheelhouse at my age. Around here it's bacon and sausages. Me, I left that behind – no wheat, no dairy, no meat – that's why I'm still going. Got to be fit to keep up with those Limousine bastards. Keeps the women interested too, know what I mean? In Frisco the women don't do age, it's just a number. You should see them in their sixties, sports car, miniskirts, boob job, hey they know how to live. Here they're darning their support stockings and praying for indulgences. Out there they live, here they think it's a fucking waiting room before they cash in their crocodile tears, thinking they fly out of the clay into the arms of some boring guy who says, "there there, everything is going to be alright". It's all just Santa Claus for adults. Well Halleluiah, give me a spell below, at least there's some action down there. Hummus', he shouted, 'this is the business. Chick peas, all that stuff. I make my own, couldn't be waiting for the local shops to catch up. Here, check it out'.

He dumps a spoon of it on an old saucer.

'Presentation a bit basic, sorry about that. My mother's stuff, can't throw it out. Anyway had to come home to plant the old man. The brother got the land and me the house, but no, his wife didn't buy into that so I tried to be reasonable, but who wants a washed-up hippy in these parts? Anyway he tried to burn the place. We all had a day out before the fella with the wig. He got a few years, hung himself in the hayshed and herself is down the road, chewing mother's little helper by the jar. I graze the land and give her a few bob, otherwise the locals would knock gaps into the place and do the Irish thing, take over I mean. Pesto, man, that's the next big thing, it's their answer to our black pudding. Any chance you'd give me a hand dosing them, the limos I mean? Takes a while to get through eighty of them'.

'I'm heading for Sligo', I say.

'Sligo, don't talk to me about Sligo. Sold my uncle's place there a year ago to a local redneck builder – four million for a field overlooking Benbulben. They built half a hotel there, now the crows are flying through it. Nice picking man, more than I ever made in Frisco on the double base. Yeah I know what you're thinking, that I'm a poof, right? Queer, is that what ye say here? Look, what people do at the weekend is their business. Me, I'm just an old-fashioned guy. Had a girl once, yeah we had plans to come over here, good place to raise kids she kept saying, but then one day a tinted Limousine – the other kind – pulled in outside our trailer, a door opened, she stepped in, a door closed and that was it. Saw her in a late night movie a few years later, wasn't pretty. Anyway, California has changed, all corporate types. The old hippies had to get out, gone up north, Portland. Only a few heads left on the street, dumped over there from the east because they can live outdoors all year round, corralled in the Tenderloin now, and a few 'Nam vets hiding with semi-automatics in the wardrobe. Ever seen *American Beauty* or

Blue Velvet? There's a lot of that stuff behind the picket fence. I wonder what's behind the electric gates here?'

It was hard to get a word in. 'Ever been to Galway?' I managed to ask, thinking I might go to Galway tomorrow, hoping he mightn't go on too long. Then I thought, why did I ask? I always end up with odd bucks who can't shut up.

'Galway, what a town, should have gone to college there. Could be a teacher in Roscommon now living on the right side of town, part of the Roscommon bourgeoisie, secretary of the tennis club, wife on the back page of the local paper winning a golf prize, holding each other up like two sods of turf in the bog – take away one and the other falls down. Galway, all water gushing from the dark plains of Mayo, a whirlpool that sucks life from Connacht, leaving only a bunch of craw thumpers dragging themselves anti-clockwise around the church in Knock like the other psychos in Mecca. Galway, where wild Connemara meets civilization, could be the San Fran of Europe if the fella above turned off the knapsack sprayer. And that catwalk between the square and the sea man puts that Ramblas place in Barcelona in the shade. If I ever went there I know I'd never leave. Saw Clapton there in Leisureland one time, what a gig. Around here you know they hate me because I have a big place and I don't play the game'.

'What game?' I enquired.

'Ah the church, GAA, Fianna Fáil, Gaeilge, circus. They wanted land off me for the school extension. Take it, I said, isn't it education? You don't have to have a hundred raffles and cake sales. Just take it, I said. Up before the bishop I was brought with a lapdog architect holding a bunch of forms and maps. One condition I told the Archbishop of Tuam after high tea and fancy biscuits in his perfectly-polished marble office. A ninety-nine-year lease for a euro and only one condition; an open school for all religions. The eyebrows lowered, meeting over. I turned back as he was pouring a brandy for himself and his sidekick.

'Where I came from in San Fran', I said, 'our gay preacher rides a Harley, looks like Dennis Hopper when he's going over the Gate. You need to turn that collar around and get a life, go to Lima and make yourself useful. Get your feet wet man instead of hiding like a dinosaur in this velvet cage'. They laughed and raised their glasses to me. I knew then that I wouldn't be getting a Christmas card from the Knights of Columbanus, so now it's back to card games and cake sales. Same with the GAA, free field for all sports in the middle of the village. No deal, so now it's race nights and quiz tables for a concrete fence around a boggy field. Ah the joys of small town life, anyway they call it local colour in the tourist brochures. I'd better be going now', I said.

It felt like I'd been here for a week.

'Thanks for the herbal tea', I said, and left the cracked mug beside the wall. 'The dampness, it'll kill you. There's a grant now to solve that kind of thing'.

'There's a grant for everything here', he said. 'A grant to get out of bed and another to get back into bed'.

I left him talking to himself. 'Good luck', I said, 'I'm off to Sligo now'.

'Good luck', he shouted and kept talking. 'L.A. don't go there, just don't go there, it used to be a great town but now, the gangs'.

I pulled the door after me. It was only twelve as I went down the steps, the Limousines had broken out again into the field from the yard and were racing around like deer.

Sligo around two seemed possible, maybe Strandhill or Rosses Point if the day held up. Good to be free, the day at my feet, mid-summer approaching. I stopped for diesel.

'Fill her up', I said as I grabbed a sandwich roll and a coffee. The Latvian man just smiled, then I noticed it was premium grade petrol going in as I paid him. It's too late now; garage owners take no responsibility.

The Latvian says I told him to fill him up. I park up and the garage man says he'll sort it out for a hundred euros but it'll be tomorrow before it's ready.

'Have you a bike?' I ask, he laughs and says I can rent one up the road.

Half twelve and I'm on the road again, Knocknarea coming into view now and a southerly wind at my back. Sligo, it will be a few hours but sure what harm. I stop in another village where there is a pile of cars outside the church. Tea and sandwiches it says, so I take them at their word and order at the bar where I read *The Farmers' Journal*.

Soon the place is full but I haven't figured it out yet. They won't take money and a pint of my choice is in front of me. It's a wedding or a funeral, haven't cracked it yet.

'Looking for a few hoggets? I'm your man', this big guy slaps me on the back, 'delivered, all paperwork in order, jewellery intact, long-eared mules, the best mothers, what do you say?'

'Don't keep mules, only crossbreds. Them mules are too soft for my wild country'.

'Where would that be?' he eyes me with an open mouth and a few black teeth like rocks in a bog, as they say.

'On the hills', I say but that's not enough for him. 'Mayo', I throw at him.

'Jesus, man you've come a long way for a funeral'.

'I was just passing', I tell him, and I enquire who's dead.

'You mean to say you took free porter and a ham sandwich without paying respects to the dead? Do ye hear that lads? We have a fella here freeloading on the back of someone else's misfortune'.

'Leave him John Joe', another one insists. 'It's not the day for that kind of thing'.

'By Jesus, I'll find out who he is', and he demands from the barman my name.

'It doesn't matter', he says, 'he's only a tramp on the road'.

'By God he didn't come here walking, but by Jesus he'll leave walking, mark my words. Respect for the dead, that's one thing my father always taught me'.

'Can I pay for the drink and sandwich?' I insist.

'Too late now, my boyo, too late. We know your type around here, don't think you can pull that one'.

The blood gone to his head now, I couldn't settle him. The barman wouldn't take anything, just pulled me aside to say leave by the back door when he's in the jacks, but he doesn't go to the jacks. He puts his arm around me and whispers into my ear.

'My boyo, whoever you are, you won't be leaving this village until you give a full account of yourself'. Then he claps me on the back. 'A man looking for good quality hoggets, no broken mouths around here, isn't that right'. He rubs his hands together. 'It's great to meet a man who's looking for quality'.

Soon the place is full, the barman shoving ham sandwiches at brawny men, debating the number of round bales you should get to the acre. I noticed there were no women to be seen. They must be across the road in the lounge bar. A tray of pints comes down but I'm excluded. I order a coffee.

'We don't do coffee'.

'Tea then?' I ask.

'We don't have a kettle', he says.

'An orange so', I say. He planks the orange on the counter and pours it into a whiskey glass. It s surrounded by the black pints.

'Tell me now', the big fella starts up again, 'over in Mayo where you're from, do they still go to the bog with the ass?' There was a loud roar of laughter. 'Velvet lugs taking half the day to get there depending on his mood', he then imitates the donkey. I sip the orange as big fella eventually heads for the jacks.

'Anyway lads', I say, 'tell me about the dead man. Did he keep hoggets?'

'No', one says, 'twenty sucking cows'.

'Well men', I say, 'It's time to hit the tar'. I thump the counter hard, finish my orange and leave fast.

It's nearly three in the day as I escape. Knocknarea looks closer now, a cap of cloud over it, the rain might hold off I think as the wind pushes me in top gear on the main road. Will be in Sligo soon, I reassure myself. The place is busy, schoolchildren in uniforms and women in cars chasing around the town looking to scoop them up. A bunch of tall bucks knock me off the bike. Psycho is in town, they say. They kick the bike and try to pull it off me to throw it in the river. I clench my fist at them. The school bus driver is laughing at me, I can see him and soon the traffic builds up. The bike is bent and punctured before the girls chant 'psycho' and one bends over to show me her thighs. Soon they all load onto the bus, the traffic moves on and the town is dead again. It was my own fault, hit town at the wrong time. Anyway it was time for high tea, I thought to myself, and a bit of fine art.

I checked out the Yeats paintings. I like the Boland funeral one, but it's the one where the two figures are sheltering as the horseman passes that interests me. What I like about it is the sky, the flying squall, the way Yeats captures it. I treat myself to tea and cakes before checking into a hotel. It's an old place full of paintings of Lough Gill and men fishing somewhere. There's a couple of tweedy types at the bar.

'Pardon me', one asks, 'do you know if Lissadell House is open? Geoffrey and I shall go there tomorrow'.

She assumes I'm working there. There's nobody else around except an old guy with a handlebar moustache reading *Horse and Hound*.

'I say', he beckons to me, 'can we have some more turf on that fire'. I throw on a few sods. I'm given a room in the penthouse suite, it seems there is nobody staying there this weekend. I have dinner with the old guy.

'Brezhnev was a total drunk, worse than Yeltsin, we couldn't get him to stop at Shannon, not like the other buffoon who couldn't get off the plane. MI5 were sharp in those days. We got Che off though, he thought there was no connection. We made sure there was none, so off he toddled into Ennis for the night, with me posing as a Labour candidate for Ennis council. Oh I knew my stuff and the Labour dream for small farmers in Clare, nationalizing the banks, the proposal to build fifty houses in St Mary's Avenue for old people. He was impressed with my vision – Che all beard and idealism – I hit him with the left wing froth and he swallowed it whole. Soon after a few pints laced with a bit of powder he sang like a canary. On his way back from meeting Khruschev we learned a lot about their plans, well Kennedy needed to know. My job was to be Peter Slattery from Ennis Urban District Council, while the real Mr Slattery was busy proposing the purchase of three mobile sheep dipping units at the sheep dipping sub-committee meeting of Clare County Council, despite the fact that there were no sheep in the town of Ennis.

'And tell me Señor Guevara', I asked, 'would your country be interested in helping us fight British imperialism on our little island?'

Che sat back and smiled with the big cigar, he wanted action, I could see. He wasn't comfortable being a minister in his new government, sitting at a desk in a glass cage wasn't Che. He couldn't drive the car when he was given the wheel. Oh no, Che preferred to be in the back seat with the gunpowder. He looked at the map on the wall. Where could they land troops, the mountains, then he smiled again. 'When I come back from Bolivia, it's nice to have a dream'.

I couldn't get a word in with this tweedy codger. It was a good job there were bones in his fish to shut him up for a while. How is it I ask myself, how is it that I get stuck with these odd types making up crazy stories, expecting me to swallow this nonsense. Full marks for imagination.

'You see, old chap', he went on, 'retired now, I don't know what to do with the day. I go to different places depending on the mood. I'm not sure how to be, anymore. The old Bentley keeps me amused, money and all that is useless. I've never been to Mayo, perhaps I'll go there tomorrow or maybe I'll go to Galway or Cork'.

I couldn't wait to see him tripping off to bed. Soon the night club opened, residents could get in free. I shuffled onto the dance floor where the crowd made space for me. It's psycho, one said and pushed me. I gave him the old one two and laid him cold. Soon the bouncer came, he didn't leave a finger on me as I retreated to the bar.

Next morning I was up at half nine, ready for the last breakfast. Met the old codger on the landing, we couldn't get down, the lift was broken. We found the stairs eventually which ended up in the nightclub. Soon we found the reception area, there was nobody there. We couldn't get into the dining room, all doors were locked except the bathroom door. We were determined to get the four course breakfast they flaunted on the menu. Soon we noticed on the security camera some people demanding and waving hands.

'No keys, let us in, we cook breakfast'.

Latvians, why does it happen to me? Is there anyone normal in this country, is it too much to ask? The old guy doesn't notice that anything is wrong. Soon they give us the menu after getting the lights on in the dining room. We carefully choose smoked salmon and scrambled eggs. After about two minutes a cremated fry lands before us with tea.

'As I was saying', continues the odd buck with the Bentley,

'You know Che, he would have made a brilliant boy scout, a natural. It's all democracy and tourism now in these countries, no fun anymore. Gorbachev messed it all up. Perhaps you could show me the road to Mayo? I understand it's quite beautiful, especially Achill'.

I took a lift with him as far as Castlebar. I had forgotten about my car as the countryside sailed by in the Bentley. Anyway when would I ever get a chance to travel in style like a Yank.

'You do know who I am', he smiled as he gave me my car keys before the big door was closed.

'Of course', I said, 'Mr Slattery', I winked, with a knowing smile.

'And you Mr McHale. Who are you?'

'When I find out', I said, 'you'll be the first to know'.

Snow

It had been freezing for over a week since the wind backed to the east.

'When the wind comes from behind the mountain it's a bad sign, that's where it was before the big snow in 'forty seven. It's coming all the way from Siberia', Heneghan kept saying that week.

Siberia became his nickname.

'As long as it stays dry I don't care how cold it gets', was always his father's reply.

Everyone in the village had a different fear of the weather, and the boy could mimic all of them. The gaps, normally a soup of mud, were seized by the continuous frost, so much so that even the cows' hooves could not penetrate it and they nervously slid from the black fields to the yard when they heard the boy clang the bolt of the heavy red gate after school. Even the pit of potatoes could only be opened with a pickaxe and had to be carefully sealed again making sure the rushes, which kept them insulated, were put back in place. It was while he was closing the pit he noticed an old man cycling to the village, his hair had turned white around the edges with the frost.

'Is them Records or Pinks?' the man enquired. 'They look like Pinks. It was a great year for the Pinks but they're too big. I gave half them to the cows, there's no taste off them'.

He cycled away into the evening – this man he never saw before and would never see again.

That night, the moon, almost full, was a hard ball in the bright sky reflecting off the frost, making the landscape seem like a perfect summer day in a photograph. The boy, crumpled up under the three Foxford blankets, could not sleep as the moonlight cast a sharp cross from the window frame on his First Communion certificate. It was useless tossing from side to side under the glare so he got up and dressed. He could walk outside and down the fields in his shoes. The cows in the barn were restless too and the hens were looking sideways through the window at the sheep dog who should have been tied up.

He decided to walk to the hill at the back of the house. The boy was in sixth class now, next year he would take the school bus to the town. An only son, he was tall for his age and had reached puberty early. He often went to the hill alone but that night felt different. Looking over the plantation of spruce trees he gleaned movement in the high branches, a sure sign of a change. Out over the mountains, smooth clouds were sitting over the peaks. His father said that someone saw a car in town with snow on the roof, a strange car from the north. Then he felt a hand on his shoulder.

'There'll be snow before morning', she said in a low voice, as her dressing gown flapped against him. He smelt the cigarette smoke and felt the heat of her breasts against the back of his head.

'See those clouds, the shape of them', she pointed, 'there'll be no school. You can mind me tomorrow'.

She ran her hand through his curls as they both gazed towards the mountains. He started walking slowly back to the house knowing she'd follow, the dog cocking his leg at every gate, trying to delay the time he would be alone again and tied up in the hayshed. He got her back into the bedroom where his father, on waking up, gazed up at him.

'Where did you find her?' he asked.

'On the hill'.

'Oh', he said. 'She didn't get too far this time'.

His father locked the bedroom door. After the boy tied up the dog to the girder of the hayshed, he went back underneath the Foxford blankets. The moon had become dull and swung around behind the trees.

He woke to the sound of a gate banging off a concrete pillar. The wind was nearly at gale force and thick snowflakes were blowing in over the turf and the straw in the hayshed. The dog was shivering trying to hide but the snow had gathered on him, as the chain would not allow him to reach beyond the angle of the driving wind.

He cycled to the crossroads; there were only the tracks of his father's car and a few bikes. The master should have passed by then, but the snow was too deep and the teacher would never risk the new Ford Cortina on the quarry hill. He waited for a while but nothing passed except a man with a rope of hay on his back, who stopped to draw his breath.

'This is a great day to get rid of old hay', he beamed. 'I'd have to use this as bedding for the cows otherwise but these girls' – he pointed to the black-face sheep waiting beside a gate at a bend in the road – 'won't piss on it today'.

He swung the rope of hay over his shoulder again and headed off. There was some light in the south-east and the snow had become lighter as he dumped the bike in the hayshed and let the dog out. This was a borrowed day, he thought. Next year he'd get a lift to the school with his father on a day like this.

After he fed the cows hay in the barn and let them out, they stood in the snow, looked back at him and lifted their tails. Then he went down the fields where the sheep ran to him. They looked dirty and disappointing in the snow. He let them into another field where they could graze under hedges. His grandfather had told him where the drifts gathered. There he found two missing sheep, breathing through a hole melted in the snow. With his hands he fashioned a track out for them, one ran off but he had to haul the other across to the shelter of a bush. She seemed to be recovering there in a green patch, but he didn't have much hope for her.

Across the barbed wire fence he could see Deane's shack on the side of a rushy drumlin. There was no smoke. His father got on well with Deane; he had the best seed oats in the parish. He decided to call up to Deane as he always gave him red lemonade. There was no road to the house, only a track for the bike though the fields to a gate at the end of the tarred road. Deane had given up on the garden after his mother died and the sheep had stripped it bare except for a few thorny shrubs near the back door. He spent twenty years in Nottingham – some said he had a woman there. Mrs Quinn in the post office swore that a black lady and a child showed up in the shop one day looking for him, but Deane was gone to the bog. He never talked about Nottingham, even when he was drunk.

The boy knocked on the front door, even though he knew that Deane nailed the front door closed against the wind from November to March.

'Come in', he heard after a while. He went round the back where the door was always open. Deane was talking down from the bedroom.

'Put on the kettle, I'll be down in a minute'.

The boy filled the black kettle and lit the gas.

Deane crawled up from the centre of a huge iron bed his mother left after her, sat on the cold frame, scratched himself and scoured the room for socks. He appeared in the doorway in his vest and long johns, pointed to the red lemonade on the windowsill beside a cup of nails and a plastic bottle of sheep dose for liver fluke.

'Now you don't have to be told at this stage', he smiled.

Then he poked the embers in the grate and coaxed them to life with some black plastic from last year's silage pit. Deane had put up a picture of Marilyn Monroe above the Sacred Heart lamp after his mother died. It was the only nail in the wall.

Of the thirteen records, all singles he brought home from London in 1971, nine of them were Gene Pitney and the other four were Elvis. He put on *Love Me Tender* as he lit a Sweet Afton. The two looked out the window at the ewe the boy had rescued from the snow drift. She was kicking a hole in the snow. The needle was stuck in the groove long after the song was over when Deane asked:

'Where will you bury her?'

He cut the hard butter and wedged it between slices of white loaf.

'Will ya have a rasher with that?' he asked.

The boy accepted the white loaf, but knew it was time to go. He left back the red lemonade bottle on the windowsill beside a triangle of snow that had blown in through a crack in the glass.

'Take this with you', he pressed a spade into the boy's hand. 'You can bring it back tomorrow'.

Deane went back into the kitchen and stood watching the boy killing the sheep with the back of the spade. It kicked for a while before settling into the final form. The boy looked back at Deane as he closed the net curtain.

The boy was hungry now but he checked his mother before he took down the frying pan from the hook. She was asleep but he would have to wake her up to cook dinner for his father. The boy cooked four rashers and three sausages, washed the delph, and listened to the news. Charles Mitchell on the wireless announced that the American B52s were bombing North Vietnam. The Vietcong were in control of a city called Hue and advancing south.

Outside, the light was fading again and the brief thaw had stopped, except at the barn where the heat of the calves kept the water trickling down the gutters. The shadows of bare branches from an overgrown tree were waving across the concrete floor when he heard her coughing. Soon she would be calling 'is there anyone out there?'

He would have to cover the dead sheep, to protect it, with a strip of black plastic to prevent grey crows from attacking it; and let the cows into the barn, before she started. They had stood in a bunch all day under a bush that offered no shelter.

She was at it when he got back. It developed from a low-pitched mantra into a feeble scream. He walked into the room but she kept it up for some time after he sat into the chair in the dark corner of the room. He opened up the jars in order and counted out the twenty-three tablets and left them, with a cup of water, on her locker.

'I need two blue ones on a Thursday', she thumped the locker. 'Don't you know anything?'

The boy counted out the extra tablet with the same detachment as he had killed the sheep.

'My things', she whispered, 'get me my things'.

He gathered up what he could find on the floor and placed them in order at the bottom of the bed.

'I think I'll wear red today, it should go well with the snow', she proclaimed as she stretched her arms into the evening.

'Well don't say anything whatever you do', she challenged him as she swallowed the last of the tablets. He knew now that it wasn't safe so he began to retreat silently.

'Don't go, please don't go', she pleaded.

The room was filling now with darkness, her naked form barely visible as she rose from the bed. He always felt uncomfortable at this point, but recently a strange warmth filled him.

'It's ok, it's ok', she reassured him. 'It's normal'.

He hesitated.

Outside a sudden snow shower whipped the trees and the darkness in the room was almost complete. He looked out the window at the mountains where the moon was still shining but soon this too would be quenched. He longed to be out there on the edge of a frozen lake. He could hear a voice saying that it was normal and talking about the flowers in spring; he wasn't sure if it was in his head or not. A long time must have passed as the trees had settled again and the moonlight streaked in through the window. She was still talking when suddenly the bedside lamp came on.

'Look at me now', she demanded in that low voice. 'Look at me now'.

The boy knew not to look at her when she was like this but he was confused this time.

'Look', she knew that something had changed in him. 'Look at your mother'.

She sensed a weakness. Part of her wanted him to succumb, to share the weight of the darkness, to know what it feels like to be an earth-rod for the family. He looked out the window again at the mountains. She could see his cold profile and knew that it was useless. She threw on a dressing gown, left the bed and approached him.

'You're a gentleman, like your father', she announced proudly and straightened his shirt collar. When he left the room he could hear her sobbing, softly at first, then a huge grief overcame her as she waded through some incomprehensible remorse.

Father would be home soon, so he lit the fire, fed the cows and checked the Hereford for calving. The full moon always brought them on. He felt the tail bones and checked the udder – she'd go another day at least. He noticed the lights on in the kitchen, she must be up. It was his job to pour out the milk in the three cups and set the table. It was always beans and black pudding on Thursdays and his father would bring home smoked haddock from the fish market. When the lights appeared at the crossroads she was out to greet him, planting a lipstick kiss on his cheek. The house was warm as the boy had lit a coal fire laced with lard and a splash of diesel.

His father was in charge of a builder's yard and three pickaxe handles had gone missing but he didn't tell her; he told the boy, then he sat down to listen to her story.

The boy scraped beans into a tin bucket with a lump of suet for the dog and left them beside him in the hayshed.

He studied some Irish grammar, traced a map of Ireland from his atlas and filled in the names of all the rivers, lakes, mountains and bays. He checked the Hereford cow again before bedtime but her bones hadn't moved. His mother's father had taught him all this before he died, as his own father was raised in the town and had no interest in land or cattle. His mother was an only daughter but her father had groomed the boy in the timeless habits of cattle from an early age.

He loved the atlas and would look at it before falling asleep, turning the pages wondering if Greenland would fit into the Mediterranean or why no river flowed out of the Caspian, pronouncing the names of strange cities; Tashkent or Samarkand he would say to himself. The moonlight was again flooding the room when the atlas fell on the floor as the boy slumped across the pillow. It fell with a map of the USSR open where the boy was reading about Irkutsk. The snow settled there for months and they drove herds across Lake Baikal. Standing on the edge of the lake he now saw the man with the frosted hair again cycling out over the ice.

'Pinks', he said, 'no taste off them. I gave the big ones to the cows', and he laughed, showing four black teeth in his entire mouth.

'No', the boy tried to stop him but it was useless.

'Pinks', he laughed, 'only fit for the cows'.

Then came the man with the rope of hay.

'I'll be very popular with the girls today', he winked. 'They won't leave a wisp after them'. He clutched at his torn coat, but he too faded out over the snowy lake.

Then came Deane on a Honda 50.

'I can't turn it off', he shouted. 'She mightn't start again'.

'What's in the carrier?' the boy tried to delay him.

'Whiskey, shins for the dog and a bottle of red lemonade'.

'Can I have your records?' he shouted.

'Anytime', he said, 'take what you want except *Lovely Leitrim* by Larry Cunningham'.

'But you don't have that record', the boy shouted.

'This baby's going to cut out if I don't keep going. Mind your mother, she's special', he said and grabbed the boy's shoulder as he sped out over the lake.

Then came his father in the car.

'Did the cow calf yet?' he enquired.

'No', the boy said, 'but the bones are down. Can I get a lift into town?' The boy hoped he could steer the car away from the ice.

'No, wait for your mother. I'll get some round steak for dinner, will you boil the spuds?' He too went into the blue snow blowing in from the lake and then he was alone.

The ice was never strong enough until mid January but they wouldn't listen. Now he was desolate with nothing but the whine of the wind for company. He had decided to walk to Irkutsk when he saw a shadow coming towards him. It was her. He stood in front of her but she walked through him. He stood again, but it was pointless. She held out her hand.

'My things', she said, 'get me my things'.

She dropped them one by one as she walked out over the lake. He followed, bending, now and again, to pick them up, before she started into it:

'Is there anyone out there?' in a low voice, at first.

The Visit

It was the Christmas before my mother died. She fell in love with death that year, the same year that my life stopped making sense. She started acting strange, as if she knew. I remember it well, something changed in her after we found poor Johnny Barrett.

'Did ye not hear it on the wireless', she said, another day, 'about a man in Roscommon dead for a fortnight until someone noticed the dog wandering around the village'.

She talked a lot like that the last year, as if she had crossed over.

'Call into McHale before Christmas, you know how odd he's gone', she shouted as she scattered a half bucket of nuts into the rusty trough for the ewes. She came from that generation – my mother – working away in her eighties, skin and bone with that fierce grip on life and a proud gait that revealed an appetite to challenge hardship.

I rushed off in our people carrier to collect Marie and the kids from the swimming pool. As I checked the mirror she looked after me, the way country people do when they pretend that they didn't see you, as if to find out something from the way you leave, before she disappeared through a gap in the whitethorns. We were in a rush to Galway to see the Ideal Homes exhibition. Marie wanted to talk to the salesman on the conservatory stand. Marie wanted to go shopping in New York this Christmas with her sister Pamela. She kept on about Macy's, dropping hints until we had a row. She was cool for a few days.

We had just moved into our new dormer bungalow on the hill overlooking the town that summer. It took two years to build – builders, they come in with a heap of machinery, pour the foundations and disappear, like a dog claiming its territory the way dogs do. It's too late then, you can't go back and if you change the length of a screw that's an extra or a variation as they call it.

I hadn't told Marie yet but it cost us two hundred and fifty thousand euro and that's not including the site at seventy five. Why we needed a conservatory is beyond me, we couldn't afford the damn thing and she wanted to build it on the north side. I hadn't told her that there wouldn't be any sunlight most of the year. She didn't like to be proved wrong but I'd have to, it was my money too. We'd both have to work for thirty years and that's assuming that I'd keep getting overtime at the present rate. When I arrived at the swimming pool Marie was furious. She was adamant that we wouldn't get to Galway on time. The kids were subdued. We rushed through the small towns as she looked out the side window. I pitied Mairead especially, because she always gets car sick on the bumps outside Shrule.

We arrived in Galway anyway, the place full of neighbours from our own town – it's no wonder our place is closing down. We got to the Ideal Homes exhibition and Marie got stuck into the poor salesman. She had everything figured out, down to the colour of the blinds. She didn't talk money at all. All she wanted to know was when would they start. I enquired politely.

'Twenty five thousand euros', he said, and it would be over thirty in the New Year for that particular model if we didn't put down a deposit. I then enquired about aspect. He looked bemused.

'The way it's facing', I suggested.

'Oh that's not important', he replied condescendingly, 'we've overcome that problem'.

'Surely sunlight is relevant to a conservatory', I hinted.

'Yes and no', he dodged, as he skipped from one foot to the other. I looked at Marie at this stage. She was not impressed.

Sometimes I pitied her. She wasn't like that when we were newly married, when we lived in that rented flat over the butcher's on Main Street. That first Christmas was truly magic – we had nothing, only a few wedding presents and a Peugeot van. We hadn't spent much time together except on holidays and then we had nothing to say. We haven't been getting on too well in the other department either. I haven't told anyone yet, well who can you talk to about these things?

Galway was full of Christmas spirit, which meant the relentless ring of cash registers, a few token drunks, the choir singing carols outside Lynch's Castle and everywhere people with their fancy paper shopping bags, swinging them around aggressively, making some kind of statement, like I've been to Roches or Brown Thomas. They might only have a pair of socks in them but that was irrelevant, it was the bag that counted. The kids loved Galway though, especially the Santa in the shopping centre. I queued for at least an hour while Marie was in Body Shop. We spent a load of money we haven't got on junk that will end up in black bags with the rubbish in the middle of January before the credit card bites the backside off us – when I say that to Marie she just rolls her eyes and bangs the door. Anyway we got home before ten, the kids had fallen asleep in the people carrier.

I had to call to McHale soon, or my mother would keep nagging. They never got on in their youth but when they got old a grudging respect set in. Since my father died I often thought she liked his company, but he became too odd up there in that cottage on his own, never even went to Mass since the trouble the clergy got into in the last few years. When the kids are making their Communion and Confirmation you can't be awkward. It's better to go along with things for the quiet life, keep it simple and don't be rising dust I always say. Sure most of us only go for the fashion parade anyway to keep the women happy but not McHale. He had to take everything serious.

'How could you be associated with the church after what they done?' he said. 'It goes right to the top', and he pointed his finger towards the ash tree outside his front door.

He only let a few people into the house that Christmas. He became more obstinate as he grew older. Looking back on it I suppose that last Christmas we visited changed me, changed us, I mean.

Anyway, I went off to work that next morning at half past six; those dark mornings were so depressing. Our place was winding down that year too; no orders came in. It was a good job I left and went on the buildings with the brother-in-law or we'd have to sell the house. When I came home we all decided to go up to McHale. Marie vowed we wouldn't stay long as she had to go to Galway again tomorrow to buy more presents and put the deposit down on the conservatory. We turned up into his road, a long narrow track with high stone walls on either side. Marie was afraid we'd scratch our people carrier.

We parked outside the cottage, knocked on the door. There were no lights on. Peculiar, I thought. They used to say that he was so mean with the electricity that he used to turn on the light to find the candle. We knocked again, no reply. Jesus, I thought, we hadn't seen him for a fortnight.

Mother was right, someone should be checking on him, you never think it'll happen on your own doorstep. Then suddenly there was a shuffle in the bushes and this form appeared with a gun pointed towards us.

'Is this what ye're looking for?' he shouted, as he threw an old copper spraying machine towards us. He must have mistaken our new people carrier for a Toyota Hiace, the tinkers' taxi as they call it.

'It's Marie and Peter', Marie shouted, 'you stupid oddball'.

McHale left down the gun and ran towards us.

'I'm sorry'.

'I'm sorry, are ye alright? I'm sorry', he kept saying, until we had to tell him to stop saying I'm sorry. The kids started laughing nervously and mimicked him in the people carrier for weeks after, laughing each time. When the dust settled we discovered he had locked himself out but he got in through a bedroom window and finally let us in through the front door.

'I saw this van coming up the road', he said, 'and I grabbed the double-barrel and waited in the hedge'.

'That's our new people carrier', Mairead shouted.

'It looks like a van to me, they all look the same', McHale laughed.

It wasn't long before the drink was out, a tumbler of Paddy which I had to drink and a sherry for Marie. He had the lemonade too for the kids.

'I don't drink lemonade', Mairead interrupted. 'I only drink Diet Coke'.

Mairead was only ten and on a diet already. Out comes the biscuits then, the tried and trusted USA. He had a good fire down, with the sheep dog sprawled in front of it.

'What do you think of Roy Keane?' Mairead asked.

'I couldn't care if he landed on Mars with the Pope on the back of a Honda 50', he declared. The kids laughed out loud.

His nephew used to send him records from America and CDs in recent years. He was big into the music, it kept him going, and the reading, always raving about some writer or another, and poetry too. Sure I never read a poem since I left school and the only one I remember was by Shakespeare, something about daffodils. The only flower I was interested in at school was Bridgie McCarthy, she was some tulip.

He had the place done up for Christmas, fair play to him, he cut his own tree and had his own holly. The decorations were from the seventies though, ridiculous paper things hanging from the light bulbs. He showed us the new CD player he got with these huge speakers and the latest CDs the nephew sent him from Boston. He had no TV that I could see and the place was paved with books.

'Did you ever hear tell of Bob Dylan?' he asked. Well who didn't? But fancy him being into that kind of stuff – a bachelor from the sticks smelling of cow dung and nicotine. Usually the middle-class hippies from the sixties who have now swapped their long hair for briefcases are the ones who understood what he was on about. He played one I never heard before called *The Hurricane*, powerful stuff sure enough, and then he played *Desolation Row*, a long rambling song. I was lost and Marie was getting impatient.

'Where did you buy the wallpaper?' she asked before the song was over. I could see that he was saddened, but I tried to concentrate on the music. The kids at this stage were halfway through the tin of biscuits and were kept amused by the sheep dog. We didn't have a dog.

'Hairs everywhere, unhygienic', Marie said. Then he put on another CD, a fella by the name of Tom Waits, something about a hooker in Minneapolis, great song but I wouldn't be shouting about it if I got a Christmas card from a whore. Marie tried to divert him by talking about the curtains and how well they matched the couch but I sensed something was going on. He never behaved like this before.

'How do the angels get to sleep when the devil leaves his porch light on?' he kept saying. He was always withdrawn. All he'd ever say before was that's the way, or you might be right. He was behaving like my mother that year before she died, acting with that embarrassing honesty, telling us about himself as if it didn't matter anymore, as if he too knew that he wouldn't be around much longer. Maybe that's the way we're supposed to live, to be direct and honest, but I'm not sure if that would work. You probably would be dismissed as the village idiot. The Yanks are a bit like that, telling you their life story the first day you meet them but they seem to get away with it. I felt a bit uncomfortable.

He said he'd have lived life differently, how he should have gone to London with his brother in the sixties and met women or gone to Chicago where his sister lived, but he was chosen to run the farm. Sometimes he said that he regretted looking after his mother until she died ten years ago. How he was too old then to do anything and how he had rotted away in a damp house without the comforts that an old man should have, because he wasn't selfish enough to think of himself.

'I was a fucking pleaser, that's what annoys me most and I've nobody but myself to blame and now what have I got to show for it – nothing but a sheep dog who's as full of arthritis as myself, hardly able to cock his leg against the gable of the house'.

Marie tried to settle him down, didn't like the f word to be said in front of the kids.

'You have your nieces and nephews and your neighbours and us, we all love you', she insisted as she recoiled from the approaching collie.

'Don't mind me', he said, 'I'm gone a bit daft lately but if I had it to live again, I'd think of myself for a change. That's what makes people unhappy', he looked up at me for some reason.

'Kids, have more lemonade', he demanded, 'there's plenty more where that came from'. Then he remembered to calm down. It wasn't like McHale. It's as if old age had stripped the clothes off him and he didn't care.

He was running around the room playing tracks from CDs I'd never heard of, Leonard Cohen, Led Zeppelin, the Beatles, then he started on the heavy stuff, Tchaikovsky, Chopin and Bach.

Marie at this stage was playing with the kids in the sitting room. She was a bit tipsy after the sherry and seemed to have lost the usual tension. I was fairly throwing back the tumbler of whiskey, something I never do but I didn't care, I was tired of talk about Macy's and conservatories and envied McHale's simple life. Everything seemed different. I felt some kind of harmony, something I never experienced in our place. I was trying to express how I felt to McHale when I said:

'I know something is happening but I don't know what it is'.

His eyes lit up.

'I knew you were a fan', he laughed, whatever that meant.

I looked out the window. It was a full moon alright, the branches of the trees were waving, casting wild shadows over the garden. Then Marie entered. She kissed me. The kids were in the spare room thankfully and McHale was busy looking for more whiskey.

'Ye can stay in the spare rooms', he said.

'It's fine', I said, 'we should be going home'.

'Stay', he insisted, 'didn't my sister have to stay in yer place once before. I had the rooms decorated the time she and her family came back from Chicago for the mother's funeral. I'll put on the heat now and the electric blankets. Them Yanks love the heat. It should be warm in an hour. Ye can't go driving home now in that condition'.

What had got into Marie, I wondered, mind you, I wasn't complaining. It had been a long time since she kissed me like that. We put the kids to bed in one of the spare rooms in a big double bed – not before something special happened.

'Did ye ever hear of the poet Paddy Kavanagh?' McHale addressed the children.

'He's on the Leaving Cert, I did', Peter my eldest son replied.

'What's your favourite poem?' he enquired.

'I can remember only two lines from *The Hospital*', Peter replied shyly.

He cleared his throat and became nervous, as if the power of the words might be too strong for him.

'For we must record love's mystery without clap trap, snatch out of time the passionate transitory', he uttered in a low voice, his face flushed with a huge smile.

Imagine our Peter on about poetry. I never suspected him into that stuff. Marie was visibly impressed, McHale shook his hand.

Then Sinead our second piped up, 'I know another Kavanagh poem' and she grabbed the book off McHale and read *A Christmas Childhood*. I heard it before, years ago somewhere. Marie and I sat on the couch beside each other as she began. There was silence after she read it. Marie was holding my hand tightly. McHale was looking into the fire for a long time. Then a tear rolled down Marie's cheek. McHale said 'well, that's the way' before he put the fire guard up. He went to bed without another word and the kids too seemed to know, the way kids do, that words were useless and scurried off to the spare room. Marie and I were different, we weren't like this since the first year we got married. We retired into McHale's other room, the full moon cast long shadows across the big double bed. We looked down over McHale's rushy fields, across the lake. Four old cows were lying under bushes beside the river. As we embraced, we said nothing, we didn't have to.

Next morning the kids woke us early. McHale was already up feeding the cows.

'We have to go to Galway to see the conservatory man', Mairead – the ten-year-old – kept repeating as she jumped up and down on McHale's huge iron bed. Marie didn't seem enthusiastic. I thought she was sick, she didn't say anything. McHale cooked up a big fry for everyone with loads of toast.

'No woman, no fry', he kept saying.

We left for our own place after McHale gave the children presents wrapped in the *Farmers' Journal*.

'Sorry about the wrapping', he kept saying and he presented us with a bottle of Power's and Harvey's Bristol Cream.

We never went to Galway that day. In fact, we never bought that conservatory. Marie was different that Christmas, something changed that night in McHale's house. It was as if my life stopped making any sense. When I found him on my birthday, that night fell into place, the way he was behaving, I mean. I noticed the cows lowing for a day or two and then the penny dropped. It was a small funeral, we finally met the nephew. He had the gait of McHale but he was a lot taller. The place went on the market a month after. Marie and I bought it, of course, borrowed every penny. We stay there some nights, especially in summer, but it is never the same as that night before Christmas. It's as if when he died that he brought something with him. I was thinking about him the last morning going to work in the dark as the lights for another Christmas were being strung across the main street of our small town. The oddball McHale – whatever he had, the rest of us are trying to create, but I don't think we'll ever get there. It's as if you have to give up something to be like him and I don't think Marie is ready for that yet. To be honest neither am I.

The Buck at the End of the Road

We were sent tarring this gravel track last year under the mountain. It seems that the road was a public road and was tarred before, but nobody important lived on it so it was ignored for years. The bushes were almost meeting in the middle. We weren't sure if anyone lived in the shack at the end.

On the Friday of the third week we saw this buck walking through the fields with a black suit and a bow tie. He had this black case with him that had a peculiar shape. To see this buck walking through the fields with wellingtons and a suit was comical surely.

'John Joe', I said. 'Look'.

Well, when John Joe looked he fell back on the chips laughing. We could see him through the bushes. He came out on the lane again below where we were working and swapped his wellingtons for a pair of shiny black shoes he had in a plastic bag.

'Oh', says John Joe. 'Who's going to the ball tonight?'

It was a wet spring and we should have been rid of that job weeks before, but every morning rain and more rain. We had this old council caravan with a stove in it and as we were over twenty miles from home we got the allowance which was tax free so we were in no rush. Only for that the job would be useless to us. Every night we went into town. It's nice to be in a strange town. We could misbehave a bit without word getting back to our own village.

John Joe pulled a few women too but when they heard we were working for the council they just laughed. I think it was the caravan that put them off. It was tricky trying to look good coming out of a caravan. We had run out of clean clothes. John Joe started to wash socks and shirts and put them on the bushes to dry. We were parked at the crossroads. It was no wonder we couldn't make progress with the women. Sure we couldn't get a crease in the trouser but John Joe did his best with the Brylcream in his hair to offset the baggy clothes. He brought home this young blonde one night. I had to stay outside for a while. It seems she was into the horses. Anyway the following morning the guards were knocking on the caravan. They assumed we were travellers and we had to move on. We couldn't convince them otherwise. They knew about the woman.

Mrs Ward who owns the Greenacres B&B told her husband, Councillor Ward, to complain that she was losing business. We would have to move the caravan back to the county council yard in the town, reducing our allowance, but John Joe wasn't going to move. That cunt Ward, he kept saying, he'll probably come down here someday congratulating us on the great work we are doing, how his money is keeping us in the job and getting the road done, while he is getting the cops to move the caravan and Brussels is paying for the job. Wasn't it him who accused our lads of putting molasses in the potholes instead of tar so he could make a laugh out of us and gain votes from the boys who, as someone said, pontificate from the high moral ground of the bar stool.

We had made great progress the first few weeks, got all the grass cleared off the old track, for that was all it was, and got the drainage almost sorted. We would soon be ready for tar, but we had to deal with Reilly.

'Ye can't let all the water into my field', he demanded.

Reilly had opened a new gap into his field near the shack and he was now driving his new John Deere tractor up the lane every day. Before, he used the gate off the main road. We had opened new water tables to allow the water to run off and to prevent flooding. After a night's rain the road was blocked with the flood.

'What about that buck at the end of the road? Why can't ye let the water into him?' he insisted. 'He's only an old foreigner anyway'.

'The house is lower than the road, sure it will be in the front door', I explained.

'There'll be no water going into my land', shouted Reilly and he blocked the water channels each night after we opened them.

There was no solution in sight, so I got the boss out from Castlebar. Reilly met him at the end of the lane; all we heard was a bit of shouting from Reilly as he walked away. The boss came up to us and started asking us about Reilly and the buck at the end of the road.

'Sort it out as best ye can', he said, 'but get the water off the road, the money is running out so finish up as soon as ye can. It's a special grant from Brussels to improve the road into the oak wood; it seems they want to get tourists walking in this way'. The boss is a nice man and he has big things on his mind. I hate annoying him with small rubbish but there was no way around it.

At the end of the third week we had run out of work. We couldn't tar the road until we got the flood sorted. The boss came out again to see if the buck at the end of the road might let the water into his place. We knocked on the door but there was nobody in. We didn't know if he had a woman or not but the place seemed very tidy. He seemed to have great work done in the garden too; he was growing all his own vegetables.

'Keep an eye out for him', said the boss, 'we have to finish the job this week'.

We had to bring the boss on the dumper as he had trouble getting through the worst of the flood too.

The boss always talks about Mayo football when we meet first, I suppose he's trying to break the ice, but he goes on too much sometimes. He must think that all council workers are GAA fanatics. It's a bad sign when he does that as we always know that there's trouble. He seems to think that we care about Gaelic football. It hasn't dawned on him yet that we're not listening. We don't care if Mayo never won an All-Ireland. I'm a Man U fan and John Joe's into Connemara ponies.

The rain was relentless that spring and the track stayed flooded. There was no sign of the foreign buck that week but we did see Reilly every day, reinforcing the dam along the side of the road preventing the water escaping into his field. We could do nothing, only playing cards in the caravan and listening to Larry's *Just a Minute Quiz* on the transistor.

It was the following Tuesday, as we were about to finish up and lock the caravan and heading for the Travellers Inn when we saw the buck in the black suit and bow tie again putting on the Wellingtons and walking though the fields.

'Hello', said I, shouting though the bushes at him.

'Hello', he shouted back, but he kept walking towards the shack.

'Come on John Joe', said I, 'we'll have to meet this buck'.

We knocked on the door twice.

'Coming', we heard. When the door opened we saw this tall thin blonde man stooping to greet us. 'Hello, you are welcome', he said in a funny accent. 'I would like to thank you for the excellent work on the road', he smiled. 'Come in, it's cold'.

John Joe and I went into this amazing place. It looked like a cow barn on the outside with grass growing on the roof but he had it completely done up inside. You could see that he was big into his music, stuff I never heard of, and a fiddle left on the table.

'What was the weather like recently?' he enquired, 'I've been away'. He must have been a long time away, I thought, as there was a pile of letters inside the door on the floor.

'Very much on the Irish side', John Joe replied.

'I pity the postman trying to get through that flood', he said.

'What parts were you in?' John Joe asked.

'Mainly Berlin, but I spent a week in Copenhagen, very cold'. He mimicked a shiver.

'You seem to like the music', John Joe ventured.

'That's what I was doing, playing the fiddle with the quartet'.

I liked the way he called it a fiddle instead of a violin as if he was trying to include us. It wasn't long before the table was cleared and the coffee ready. The walls were covered with paintings and prints. There seemed to be only one bedroom upstairs with a balcony, all the other rooms were all knocked into one with a small bathroom extension beside the back door.

'Do you find this old house damp?' asked John Joe.

'I'm slowly getting used to it', he said, 'but when I'm away it takes a long time to heat it up again. I'm hoping to dry-line it and insulate it this year'.

It seemed very cosy to me even though it wasn't awful warm.

'Being lower than the road doesn't help. Where does all the water from the roof go?' I enquired.

'Into a barrel at the corner, I use it for washing and in the garden but sometimes in winter I have a flood'.

'That's why we're here', said John Joe, 'I suppose you don't need any more water'.

'Definitely not'.

'Well you see we have a problem on the road with water and we were hoping that you might be able to help us'.

'Of course I'll try', he said, 'anything to give the poor postman a dry road'.

John Joe put forward this idea that we would pipe all the water into the foreigner's garden off the road and make a soak pit down the bottom of the garden which would also help to dry the garden and the ground around the house. He agreed, to my surprise. I wouldn't allow it in my garden and John Joe certainly wouldn't either but I could hear my boss' voice in my head saying, 'solve it as best ye can lads, we have to finish here this week'. I could see now that John Joe was itching to get away to see the blonde horsey woman in the Travellers Inn now that we had the deal done but we'd have to get him to sign an agreement.

'We'll go ahead with that so and the boss will get you to sign up the paperwork this week. Will you play a tune for us when the job is over?

'I'll play one now', he said and took up the fiddle. 'It's by Vivaldi, but that doesn't matter, it's called Spring'.

'We could do with a bit of that', John Joe interrupted.

'Yes', he smiled. He paused before playing as if music could start only through the breaking of silence. It was all a bit above my head but he was certainly handy with the fiddle. John Joe was impressed too but now that the deal was done he just wanted to keep him on side until he was signed up.

'You remind me of Yehudi McManamon. I saw him on the box one night', said John Joe.

'You are very kind', he replied, 'perhaps you were thinking also of Stephane Grapelli, he played with Yehudi'.

'One of them anyway', John Joe complemented him again.

The next day before we started we saw Reilly and Councillor Ward; Reilly as usual waving his hands and Ward agreeing with him, saying it was a disgrace. Then Ward came down to us, told us to let the water into the foreigner's garden. I told him that I'd have to talk to the boss first. I knew that Ward didn't care about the buck as we called him, because as Ward put it, 'them foreigners never vote'. He probably checked the voting register before he came out to make sure that he wouldn't lose a vote.

'This man', Ward went on, 'this man has worked hard all his life to rear his family and can't afford to have water on his land from the road'.

'But that's where it was always going', I told him, before the road was neglected.

'He's a good family man. His mother is sick, and he's chairman of our sheep dipping committee in the Council this year. We have to look after our own'.

He spoke loudly so he could be heard by Reilly. If we didn't solve the problem he threatened that he'd be on the local radio, that he'd talk to the county manager and that he'd write to the Minister for the Environment.

That day we started piping the water towards the buck's garden. Reilly was hugely impressed, thinking that Ward had bullied us into doing the job, walking up and down the lane, his hands held together behind his back whistling some dumb tune. At lunchtime he went home on the tractor but was back again at two o'clock claiming to be fencing along the track but in his self-appointed supervisory role.

We had just finished piping the water to the foreigner's gate when we saw the door opening.

'Come in out of the cold', he insisted. We brought in our sandwiches laden with cheese and ham but he had a smoked salmon salad prepared for us with a pot of coffee.

'We have a new boss', John Joe broke the ice, but the foreigner didn't understand.

'Your neighbour', John Joe clarified.

'Oh, Mr Reilly', he nodded.

'And Ward, the politician, with his suit and tie, telling us something we never knew'.

'What's that?' the buck looked confused.

'That water must obey gravity'. The foreigner smiled but was unsure. John Joe was fairly angry with Ward as he was still trying to get our caravan moved away from the crossroads near his wife's B&B. It seemed that himself and the blonde gypsy were barred from the Travellers Inn the night before. The 'Tinker's Enemy' he kept calling it that day.

Then we heard this knock on the door. It was the boss. I got up as there were only three chairs in the room and left a chair free for him. The boss looked a bit odd in this old house where he to had to stoop to get through the door. He started talking about football immediately.

'Oh Mayo should have taken off Barrett at half time'.

He was talking animatedly for a good while when he noticed that nobody was listening, except the foreigner who was too polite and asked him was it Gaelic football or soccer. There was a silence then while myself and John Joe kept our heads down. It was slowly dawning on the boss that he must be a foreigner. Then suddenly he remembered that he had to get a signature so he started asking the foreigner about music. The boss isn't into classical music, except maybe for the Blue Danube.

'I like Strauss', he said, but I knew that this was the only classical music he knew, the same way as he talked about Georgie Best and soccer.

'What kind of music do you like?' asked the foreigner.

'Neil Diamond', he replied, without hesitation.

'Oh, *The Beautiful Noise*'.

'That's my man', said the boss, clenching his fist with that sad middle-aged lack of conviction. This was all the foreigner knew about pop music, I could tell, judging by the CDs and posters around the room. 'But my wife is into Barry Manilow', our boss ventured as if that might rescue the situation.

'Do you give lessons, because my daughter is trying to learn the violin and it's impossible to find anyone? They're all booked up. It's a bit like trying to get my other daughter into the Gaelscoil'.

'We'll soon have an Irish-speaking orchestra', says John Joe, but I knew this was not what the boss wanted to hear. He is chairman of the tennis club now. I saw him in the *Connaught Telegraph* so I always ask him about the club and how he sees the club going forward in the new millennium.

A long time ago I learned that you should find out what the boss wants to hear and keep saying it.

'Isn't it great', I said, 'that they want to speak the language. In my time it was bet into us. They must be very bright altogether, a bit like their father'.

He smiled back at me indulgently.

'Well I don't know about that'.

'I would be glad to give your daughter lessons when I'm not away, but it's difficult being so far out of town', the buck said.

'Well the road will be better now if we can solve the water problem and you might get more business if people could get here easier, which is why I'm here'.

The boss pulled out a form and a map out of the file. He explained that the only way to prevent the road from flooding was to pipe the water into the foreigner's garden and dig a soakage area to dry the garden. The foreigner signed the form and the map and thanked the boss profusely for solving the flooding problem.

'Play an old tune for us before we go back to work', John Joe squinted up at the fiddle.

'This is a lively sonata from Paganini', the foreigner replied.

'Another Roscommon full-back', said John Joe. The boss laughed. It was the most beautiful music I had ever heard.

'Jesus, he can play the fiddle', John Joe said outside the house as he pushed his jumper inside his trouser to stop it falling down.

'The violin', the boss corrected him. The boss was whistling *Beautiful Noise* as he thanked us for setting up the foreigner to sign the form and of course he had a violin teacher for his Leaving Cert daughter.

I noticed Ward and Reilly at the end of the lane waiting for the boss. They all spent a while together joking, laughing about football. We didn't pretend to hear them but I knew that everyone was happy now and the job was going ahead – even Reilly, despite the fact that his mother was dying, conceded a smile. Soon Ward appeared.

'Jaysus ye're mighty men altogether, where would the Council be without ye. Some fellas in them offices talk about work, but ye do it. Isn't that cunt Reilly awkward about the water, but don't say I said that. Wouldn't you think the engineer from Castlebar would put him in his place'.

We piped the water into the foreigner's garden that week, buried a few loads of stone at the end of the pipe and began to cover the lot with a veneer of soil before we seeded it. There would be a nice coat of soft grass over the garden in the autumn and hopefully that would be the end of the problem.

The boss didn't waste any time either. His Mercedes pulled into the foreigner's yard two days after the deal was signed with his daughter. John Joe and I were finishing up in the garden when we saw them. The girl was small and shy, dressed in a tracksuit top with a printed logo *Harvard*. She wore jeans and runners but her eyes were like those of an Indian woman, big and dark. The girl dismissed her father. She was glum and withdrawn and told him to call back in an hour.

We were working overtime to finish the job but the rain every day was relentless. I knew that this job would spell trouble if we couldn't spread the topsoil and seed the garden. When the boss returned he knew too that if the garden started flooding that an alternative solution would be impossible to find. All the land around the foreigner's house was owned by Reilly and there would be no compromise there. Then suddenly the boss' daughter emerged, laughing.

'Thanks', she kept repeating, as she toned down her reaction on approaching the car. The boss rubbed his hands together.

'Finish up, lads, as quick as ye can, even if ye have to work on Saturday'.

He winked at us and nodded at the house. We would have to cut the bushes too, the boss said, before the first of March because of the birds' nesting, otherwise the lunatics in the wildlife department would have us all locked up.

The boss manoeuvred the Merc several times in a mucky gap and eventually she moved slowly down the lane; the branches pulling at the mirrors.

We had to abandon the job in the foreigner's garden. The water gathered at first in a corner, then crept over the soakage area and eventually one morning it was, as the foreigner described, 'splishing at the back door'. The last full day's work we had done was washed away by the flood and the chippings off the road were gathered in a pile beside the house. When the boss came with the daughter he left quickly.

We noticed the girl was changing with each lesson. She seemed more vibrant.

'Hello fellas', she chirped at us before knocking on the door. She was dressed different too, with a pink t-shirt, black skirt and shoes with a strong heel. 'Did you see Lars today?' she enquired.

'No we didn't see much life at all yet, but them musicians keep funny hours', John Joe seemed to be warning her. She left the fiddle on the window sill and walked round to the back door and knocked again, calling his name several times. Then she threw stones up at a window which was probably the bedroom. Soon a muffled reply came.

'Sorry I forgot, I was playing late last night, come in Pamela'.

She pushed in the back door avoiding the flood now lapping in gentle waves against the back wall of the house. The house remained in darkness except for that one room. When the boss called back she was still there. He too knocked on the back door but we pretended not to see. When he got around to the front door again she was waiting. As he approached the car she grabbed the fiddle without him seeing. Then John Joe went up to the boss.

'What do you recommend we do? There's not much point in doing anything until things dry out'.

The boss sent us to a new job nearby but told us to check it every evening and report to him.

'Daddy', she accused, 'what about the flood around Lars's cottage. It's not fair, why did you do this, how could you exploit a poor musician?'

John Joe and I turned away and pretended to be doing something. The boss couldn't say a thing because he knew she was right.

I was down there a few weeks after, checking the flood which by now had surrounded the house. The foreigner had blocks thrown in the water using them as stepping stones into the house. The boss arrived with the daughter so I stepped into the bushes. She tiptoed to the front door as the boss drove away. The foreigner opened the door and she hung her arms around him. They disappeared as he carried her inside.

Reilly came down the road, swaggering, whistling some tune triumphantly, trying to claim the evening.

'Will the new moon bring a change? This rain has everywhere swamped. I can't let out the cattle even though there's plenty of grass. It's nothing but drawing rolled barley from the Co-op. It's costing me a fortune. Look at the foreigner's garden, it takes awful rain to leave it in that state. Isn't it a shame, and that was a beautiful cottage when old Mrs Walsh was alive. I hear he's some class of a musician'.

'How's the mother?' I asked. 'I haven't seen you for over a week'. I knew she had to be very low.

'Ah, it's only a matter of time now, she doesn't recognize us anymore. She won't last long now'.

He was right sure enough. It was a huge funeral, Reilly had a large family. The foreigner showed up too which was very unusual. He was never seen at mass, in fact I don't know which foot he kicks with. I was talking to him outside the church, he didn't seem to know anyone else.

'I could play music tomorrow at the burial service', he offered, 'our quartet is playing at the local arts centre'.

'A change is long overdue', I encouraged him.

'Call me Lars', he insisted as he offered to shake my hand. I found it funny calling someone Lars but it seems it's like our Larry. That's what I like about the job, meeting strange people.

'I'll mention it to Reilly', I said, knowing that Reilly was too proud to ask. I invited Lars to the pub, where I could meet Reilly and suggest some classical music, that it would be a fitting tribute to his mother instead of the school choir. His brothers and sisters from Dublin were enthusiastic but Reilly remained unconvinced.

'It has to be the best, I never heard that buck playing', Reilly insisted.

I called over Lars to meet Reilly's family. He suggested a number of pieces but nobody ever heard of them except Reilly's sister who was living alone. She qualified as a teacher but ended up working in a library.

'Albinoni, I'd like him to be played at Mum's funeral'.

She was being ignored but she said it again, louder.

'Albinoni's *Adaggio*'.

The foreigner's eyes lit up.

'It would be a privilege. It's one of our favourite pieces in the quartet', he replied.

Reilly knew nothing about the music but he knew enough to agree with his sister when she was persistent about something, which was seldom. She wrote down the three pieces to be played for the leaflet she would have printed off for the mass.

The following morning the church was crowded; it was the first fine day in about three months. The Reilly's and their extended family from Killiney in Dublin took up about half the church seats. The priest sat down after delivering the usual comments about a long and happy life with her family and how important the church was in her life. Slowly the sound of the violins filled the church. The priest looked a bit shocked as he never saw Lars before. They played for a good while, and you could hear a pin drop in the crowd. Afterwards nobody knew what to do, even the priest seemed confused. Then Reilly's sister stood up, clapped and slowly everybody joined in, to save her embarrassment.

Reilly was slow to stand up but he had no choice. His sisters were hugging each other before they sat down again. After the communion he played again; a piece called *Meditation from Thais* by Massenet, it said on the leaflet. As we left the church he finished with another piece called *The Lark Ascending* by a fella by the name of Vaughan Williams.

Outside everybody shook Reilly's hand and congratulated him on the music; a fitting tribute to a fine lady, Mrs Quinn, the teacher kept saying. Ward too was shaking hands with everyone

'Wasn't it mighty music altogether, who'd ever think that the foreigner had it in him'.

He sympathized with Reilly, 'I hope the road's nearly finished now, it's a fine job, I'm glad I put my money into it, them council boys are long enough at it'.

Then the boss showed up and pulled me to one side.

'What about the foreigner's flooding problem? I wonder can we do anything? Do your best. See what ye can do'.

checked the road that week. Something strange had happened, the flood had gone and all around the house a new path had been laid. When I checked the water tables I discovered that they had all been opened. That summer as the sky thickened and depressions queued in the Atlantic to cross over us, streams of water were pouring into Reilly's field.

Argentina

I always pop in to see her every morning – regular as clockwork I am. She always has that same smile; it keeps me going for the day. Then I open the curtains, turn up the Super Ser gas heater and thank God for having such a fine woman in my life. At nine sharp I bring her the breakfast but she never eats anything, even her favourite sugar-coated Krispies are always left there untouched. I pop in again at bedtime to pull the curtains and turn off the heater for the night. There's an awful smell of gas from that bloody Super Ser lately. I must bring it back to the Co-Op and get a new one. They say you shouldn't leave them gas heaters on if the door isn't open.

Then it's all action for the day, except for this morning when I woke to that sound upstairs as if someone had dropped dead on the floor. Mother would have to wait while I checked John Joe. Why I did this I didn't know, but mother would understand, she always did.

John Joe sleeps upstairs in the box room, he never left it. He still has the doll mother gave him in 1921 and a picture of Marlene Dietrich he had cut out of the *News of the World* nailed onto the wall over his bed. John Joe was a fine man in his time. Whenever a cow went into a hole up in the bog John Joe was called for. When he got on the end of the rope she was coming up. The grip was something else. During springtime he was awful popular when the cows were calving especially with them Charolais calves. Everyone wanted to have Charolais calves but since the cows were too small for them John Joe was your man. Not alone would he pull the calf but he'd also pull the cow around the barn especially if the hips were big.

'Pull towards the udder', we'd say but John Joe would pull the cow through the door, jamming the poor cow and eventually releasing the calf.

He's gone forgetful lately though. Didn't he wear the wellingtons to Mass last Sunday and the previous Sunday he served Mass just like in the old times and said all the responses in Latin. The priest took no notice. I'm worried about him lately. This morning when I pushed in the door I got a shock. He had moved the bed around again, faced it east for Christmas. That sound I heard was the four copies of the *Golden Pages* falling off the shelf. He's always reading, every year he compares the new and the old. He was all ready to go to town.

'Hurry up', he said, 'or we'll be late for the fair'.

'Sure the fair's finished ten years ago', I said.

'What'll we do with the red white-head cow?' he demanded.

'She's going to the factory on Saturday', I insisted.

You should have seen him, shoes polished and the tie on. He still looked well. It's a pity the brain is a queer thing when it starts giving trouble. He wouldn't take them off though.

'You'll ruin your clothes down the field', I said.

'We have to feed the sheep in the bog field', he demanded.

I was mad with him having washed him the night before in the bath. It wasn't easy trying to get him to lie down. He has stopped taking his clothes off too, so I had to pull them off as best I could. Drinking the water in the bath was the latest mischief and he had to have the framed picture of Marilyn Monroe and the plastic boat mother bought for him or he'd pull the plug.

I got him to put on the wellingtons when we were going to feed the sheep but he wouldn't take off the suit and tie. He liked the spin in the transport box of the tractor but I had to hide the key since he took off one night for Castlebar looking for a woman. The only thing that saved him was that he ran out of diesel before he got onto the main road. I had got used to him being ridiculous or maybe I too was going a bit daft. Who knows? Madness is only what other people decide is mad and that seems to change all the time. Say I kept going to Mass in the pony and trap like we all did years ago and didn't change to a tractor or a bike I'd be classified as a bit mad and they could lock me up. It's important to change with the times, never to be the first and never to be the last to try out something new, my mother used to say. I don't like to stand out too much but it's hard with John Joe.

The neighbours don't call to the house anymore but I see them at mass. They never ask about John Joe. It's always about mother.

'How is she? I haven't seen her for ages', they keep saying.

'What age is she now?'

'Fine', I always say. 'But she doesn't stir out much anymore. Anyway you never ask a lady her age'.

That normally shuts them up. We were due to have the Stations last year but I refused them. I knew it would disturb mother. Old grey badgers asking about her, especially her classmates from national school.

'And how is Kathleen and your dad? Is he still in America? I'm sure he will be home soon'.

They have nothing better for doing than stirring up trouble. Sure I don't annoy them about their families, that's all private stuff. The priest is the worst. He can call without notice, he keeps asking about mother, but I keep insisting that she won't leave the room and is gone odd, will only see the family.

'What about the sacraments my man'? he glares at me in that superior way.

'I'll have her ready soon, Father, next time you call', I say.

When the Yanks came back they had her taped singing *If I Were a Blackbird* and sent me back a tape recorder and the tape. She liked listening to that. We should have bought her another tape, a Bridie Gallagher one, or maybe Dana singing *All Kinds of Everything*, but we never got around to it. There was always something more important for doing.

Anyway when the priest comes I always play the tape from the bedroom, insisting that she is in great form.

'Well she sounds like a young woman', he smiles, 'but I haven't heard her confession for a long time'.

He's going a bit daft too, sure it's over ten years at least. He says the same thing every time. I suppose when you get to eighty the memory starts eating itself. I pour him a half Powers and link him into the Morris Minor.

'Remember my young man', he repeats, as he straightens himself before stooping to get into the car, 'the family that prays together, stays together'.

He revs up the old black Morris and drives in first gear all the way back to the village.

When I arrived in the quarry John Joe jumped off, filled the troughs for the sheep then opened the gate and let them in. They nearly tumbled him as they rushed to the feed.

'Two missing', he said. How he could count that fast I don't know. He was always good with numbers, knew the number plate of every car at mass, knew where they were registered.

'IR is Offaly, ZW Kildare', he'd say.

'What's Longford?' I'd ask.

'IX', he'd reply.

Sure I never had a head for that type of thing. When that Ras Tailtean bicycle race came to the village he'd have them counted sitting at the grotto as they whizzed past in groups. Seven he'd say, then thirty-two, then seventy-four. It must be counting the sheep going out a gap that made him that keen.

He then told me which sheep were missing, the lame one and the one that got maggots in August. How could you not admire a man with that ability and yet I'm a bit ashamed of him, the way the neighbours are always laughing at him. It's not right, they were like that with mother too. I think he'd be better off to stay in the house and that way I could keep the family together. I know we're a bit different but sure who knows what's going on in any family behind closed doors.

Mother went a bit odd when dad left. They say it's natural when someone you love disappears but we kept it quiet, his absence I mean. I was only six at the time. We told the neighbours that his brother died in America, that he was gone to the funeral. Then we said he had to sort out the affairs, sell his house, he'd soon be home. Soon they stopped asking. I never knew why he left. We must have done something or maybe I said something wrong. Mother always said he was very fond of the suitcase but he promised he'd be home some Christmas. We always waited on Christmas Day and left a place set for him. I was determined to mind mother, she was all we had left. I never want her to leave and me ending up going a bit odd too. It's important that someone keeps the family together and that's my job now. Nowadays with families splitting up you can end up on your own and then you'd definitely go a bit odd.

I told John Joe that we'd come back before dark to find the two missing sheep and we left the quarry for home. His suit at this stage was destroyed but he kept singing a song from the sixties, something about, I left my heart in San Francisco, it was that or John McCormack, *I hear you calling me*.

The day was easy to praise, showers sweeping down from the mountain and the floods rising in the fields. We had to move the troughs to high ground in November and we'd have to move them again before the new year. The whole place was turning into soup. The tractor too was digging two deep furrows between the quarry and the gate, where two streams poured down the hill to a small pond that overflowed into a bigger pond. If we didn't have speed built up coming into the flooded ruts she'd get stuck and we'd have to get the neighbours' tractor to pull us out. That happened one year but I hate asking for help. They'd be asking questions about mother. How she must be a great age now. They know my age and John Joe's. He's sixty nine and sure they know what age she was when he was born. They know the answers but I don't know what they're trying to get at. Sometimes they wink at each other when they ask that question. I never ask them what age their mothers are. Sure it's none of my business. Anyway I don't care.

The only one of them I trust is McGowan. He brings the cattle and sheep to the factory and always pays in cash. It mightn't be the best price but sure he has to keep that truck on the road. He takes away the dead ones too and looks after the paperwork. I never understand why cattle have to be tagged. It's all paperwork nowadays. He does the tagging for us. When we get the cheques from Brussels I give him a few bob. He's the only neighbour I meet in recent years and he knows not to ask about mother.

John Joe always hops off and opens the gate. He salutes like he used to in the LDF days. We used to get the guns then to take home in the war years. We'd practice on an old door under a hill. It was hard to get meat then but you'd never go hungry with John Joe. He had the parish fed with rabbits and when it came to foxes he fairly collected in the barracks at a shilling a tongue. When the trouble started up north they took the guns away and called us the FCA.

I parked the tractor on a hill overlooking the house, you can never trust the battery especially in January. John Joe fed the cows hay in the barn while I milked the Friesian. You never feel the day going this time of year. By the time the dinner is over, it's getting dark. The neighbours passed twice that day. Where they were going I'll never know, always in a rush. John Joe usually goes to sleep after the spuds, then I wake him up around seven. He loves to watch *One Man and his Dog*, his favourite was *Hawaii Five-0*.

That day after he went to bed around five I tidied up and walked down the land to find the missing sheep. The showers had cleared and the moon was coming up over McDonell's rushy hill. The frost was settling in and I could feel the grass tighten under my boots. The moon was nearly full and the last sunrays were clashing with some high clouds out over the Atlantic.

It's at moments like these I feel like a king but there's no one to share it with. The sky always surprises me. Just when you're fed up of wind and rain this happens. It makes me think sure there must be a God. I don't have a big farm but this is better, having the time to appreciate all this. But you couldn't go talking like that, people might think you were a bit odd. Anyway when it comes to crossing the border I'd prefer to be buried here, under the ash on the hill facing south. All that funeral fuss is a bloody nuisance.

When someone dies belonging to you it's as if something takes over the place and you lose control. I believe that the family should be allowed to do their own thing. The family should be protected at all costs. First thing the neighbours are in the door, squinting at everything in the house. It would be like having the stations, you'd have to clean the place from top to bottom and then you'd have to make them tea and offer them drink. When they'd look at the corpse they'd say nice things about it and sure they mightn't have talked for twenty years. Then the priest comes in and they cut into the Rosary. It could be two o'clock when you get them all out. It must be nice for the people to have the corpse back to themselves. I'd stay up all night because that would be the last night you'd see it.

The next day then they'd come in droves, politicians and so called friends, people you didn't know. You have no privacy, that's what annoys me. They're not happy until they take the body away in the coffin. Then it's prayers and Mass and you have to be nice to everyone. After the burial you have to buy more drink before you can go home.

That's when it hits you, no one in the room and you end up setting a place and making dinner for an extra person. I hate empty rooms, they just wreak with absence. I don't buy into all that. A man should have the freedom to do what he wants with his own as long as it doesn't affect anyone else.

I found one of the sheep in a briar, he had wrapped himself into it and had eaten a circle of grass around himself. I unwound him and let him off. I noticed another flat in the middle of the field. He seemed to be kicking at something and occasionally he'd jump up and roll over on his side. One of his eyes was missing and I knew by the grey crows on an ash tree nearby that they already had paid a visit. He kept kicking into the clay and had dug up the sod into a paste. I straightened him but it was useless. He kept beating his head off the ground and kicking. Soon he became too weak and all I could do was point him towards the full moon as it crawled up over the hill. The huge orange moon cast long shadows across the field down towards the lake as two hares played in the gathering fog. They seemed a long way off. It was as if the moon had discovered myself and the sheep.

I have witnessed death in all seasons but I never get used to it. I've buried cattle, sheep, even the donkey after he strangled himself with the rope I had tying him to a tree. It's the sadness that gets to me watching them dying and the way it colonises their eyes. The way they kick in the final agony before they settle into that final position, head outstretched as if they were trying to leave their bodies behind. It seems to me that we're improving on the living but not on the dying. It's as if once death takes over it plays with the victim in its own torturous way.

I get the vet when there's hope but sure it's always only a fifty-fifty chance. Summer's always the worst with the flies. Farmers must learn about death, they must learn to accept it. I suppose it prepares them for their own death too. Anyway I think people should be buried in their own land. Keep them as close as possible I say, and there shouldn't be any mad rush to bury them, that should be up to the family. Keep the family unit intact as long as possible. God knows there is enough of pressure on the family in modern Ireland.

There's my niece up in Dublin, sure she hardly sees her kids at all. I don't think they ever sit down together to have a family meal. It's so important to eat together and share the events of the day, the little crises that can be shared; we all know a load shared is a load halved. That's why we often have dinner in mother's room. She never says a word but then again she was never one for the talk.

By the time I got back to the house John Joe was up and outside feeding the cows. They didn't need to be fed again. What am I going to do with him? He's in good health, but he's gone upstairs. I'll have to lock him in the house soon. I can't have the neighbours laughing at him. It would be nice if we were all in the one room together like when we were small, when daddy was around. I brought John Joe in and planked him in the armchair. *Dallas* was on the TV, I think he fancied Sue Ellen. *The Virginian* was always my favourite cowboy.

I went into the kitchen to make the supper. We usually have cheese and eggs on Mondays. It doesn't take long for a life to change after which there is no going back. John Joe was no good with the new colour television. He couldn't figure out the buttons so he opened up the back of it and it turned on. He used to be good at fixing things especially the Ferguson 35 but sure times have moved on. Anyway that was how it happened. There he was with a screw driver clutched in his hand with bits of the TV round him and a blackened distorted face. I closed his frightened eyes. I noticed the lights dimming when I was boiling the eggs but I thought it was lightning. Sure how can you have lightning and frost at the same time, my mind must be going a bit too.

I ate the supper immediately, four eggs and a slice of loaf. I hate cold eggs. We don't like to waste anything in our house. The cheese would keep. It was all for the best as the neighbours might say, all over in a second. I had to clean up the mess and drag him downstairs and put him in the bath.

Then it dawned on me, the silence was terrible, having no television for the full night and then in the weeks to come neighbours asking questions about him and winking at each other when I go to mass. It's not easy keeping the family together with all that interference from outside. Anyway I left him in the bath soaking. He seemed happy now that all the torture was over. It's as if he knew that he had gone a bit too odd, like mother, and he couldn't cure himself. Every time he tried to be normal it didn't work out and the more he made an attempt the more forced it became so people avoided him.

I often think that if he had met a woman he might be more like other people. She might take the corners off him. Every time he met a woman he told it in confession, company keeping was a sin then. It was hard to meet a girl if talking to her was a sin. I suppose he was a bit like me too, comparing them to mother. Nobody could measure up to her.

After I washed J.J. – that's what they called him when he played full-back on the under-eighteens, the same team won the West Mayo Junior Final – I dried him off and put on the best suit of clothes he had. It still fitted him, never put on a pound, still straight as a rule despite the years. All that army training stood to him. For a minute I was almost sad remembering all the antics when I had to dress him after the bath but now he made no effort at mischief. It's strange how you miss people a bit even though they cause you trouble. I could never understand that. I sat down on the sofa for a while reading *The Farmers' Journal*. The price of straw was gone up to nearly a pound a bale, that's delivered, sure hay is better value at two pounds fifty. There's was a great article too on the cost of producing beef in Argentina – it's only half the cost – it's no wonder they can flood the common market with cheap meat. They have big ranches out there too where they round up the cattle on horseback.

I must have fell asleep thinking about Argentina because I dreamt that John Joe and I were out there rounding up cattle. John Joe lassoed a new calf and branded him with the experience of a real cowboy and there was another man there, a tall silent man who John Joe was taking the orders from. He looked like John Joe too. When we stopped at the timber house in the valley beside the Rio Grande, mother ran out to greet us.

'You're just in time for the dinner', she beamed up at us and we all tied up our horses and beat our big hats off our thighs. He sat at the head of the table. It was him, of course, tall, proud, silent, the way I imagined him, the way he'd be if we hadn't said something wrong, smiling at mother and she fussing with the dinner.

'Settle, woman', he'd say. I remember that from my childhood. John Joe kept saying it after he left to comfort mother, but sure it only made her worse. That was before she went a bit odd.

Something must have woken me up anyway. I think it was John Joe stiffening up falling off the couch, still up to his old tricks. I looked out, the sky was slowing filling with light, the Christmas lights in Gaughan's house were winking on and off. I lit a Woodbine thinking about Argentina and blew the smoke into the first shaft of light squinting across the room. They say there's no bottom to the soil out there, imagine that.

I brought John Joe into mother's room and sat him upright in the chair, on the other side of the bed just like the day daddy left, all back together again except for himself. I opened the door. Mother too was waiting in that timeless poise as I brought her in the sugar-coated Krispies, opened the curtains and turned on the Super Ser. The first sunrays shone on mother and John Joe. They looked happy as if free from something. I sat down again and left the armchair empty, then I closed my eyes and dreamt of Argentina. I thought I heard a door close somewhere in that lost dream. When I woke up and tried to turn off the gas, he was there as mother had promised for Christmas, smiling just like her and John Joe. We were all together at last.

At the Crossroads

Deane woke up late after drink. He threw an arm towards the noise, cleared the top of the locker, finally found the wind-up clock, silenced it. He stumbled downstairs to the hall where a single envelope was floating on a veil of water blown in under the door. Through the window in the envelope he could see his name and address in that familiar style, with the red design behind – the headage cheque. He tiptoed through the water, retrieved the envelope and tore it open. The water stain had crept over the top of the cheque but hadn't quite arrived at the number that said one thousand five hundred and eighty two pounds and forty seven pence. Fuck, he thought as he shook the water off the corners. The numbers would be blotched soon. He grabbed the two-bar electric heater, placed it on top of the table, plugged it in where the wireless plug usually goes and held the cheque facing the glowing bars. The heat was useless to his legs and back as he shivered in his underpants. All he could do now was watch and hope the water would not attack the numerals. It had already blotched the address and was about to annex his herd number. He held it upside down to invite the moisture back over the wet sections. Outside Mary McHale was looking through the net curtains beckoning him with a toothless smile.

Soon the paper became brittle as it dried and the watermark held firm just over the numerals but had invaded the words where it said five hundred. He hoped that they'd cash it in the pub and set it against his debts – there wouldn't be a lot left after paying for the beet pulp and dip. The Angelus bell from the village was echoing between the hills and spreading out across the bog before it clanged into the front wall of his damp mass-concrete house.

He never used the front door in winter as it faced west – he bolted it shut, nailed two planks across it and jammed it with a canvas bag at the bottom to prevent the water getting in. He stored the sheep feed in the scullery to protect it from rats. He coughed going out the back door the sheep answered beyond the fence. He emptied a half bag of beet pulp into the troughs as they shuffled around him in the mud. Two ducks flew away from the flooded field as the wind scarred the surface with sudden gusts. He never counted the sheep. Keep the numbers up, McGuire always said, he always had around 250. They had blackened the small fields at the back of his house where every day a couple were caught in briars or in a drain.

He noticed birds in a corner of a field where one lay half eaten and another was dead in a drain. The crows and gulls circled overhead as he bundled the carcasses into a large bag especially for the purpose. He flung the bag across his back and stumbled over the greasy mud, falling once as he climbed over a scattered wall. The rain and wind was relentless in his face as he dumped the bag at the side of the house. He went in to put on a second top coat before heading out for the bog. The crows followed him along the track up across the hill; there was no shelter except a few bent bushes in the quarry.

Saturday was a good day to dump dead animals in the bog hole as the civil servants were off work and, Deane thought to himself, them crowd from the parks and wildlife would be out sailing or climbing some mountain. He had already figured out that if you missed out on bonfire night in June to burn tyres or silage covers, a foggy day in winter would provide an adequate disguise. There was only one man who might cause trouble and that was McMillan, who had built a summer house on the edge of the bog. He seldom appeared in winter though, only around Christmas when he brought journalist friends to show them where he intended to write his novel. Deane knew that his septic tank was leaking into a drain and would allude to it sideways in conversation with McMillan, saying, with a wink, that we were all in the same boat around these parts.

In the distance he could see the crossroads. From the east, McGuire was heading towards the bog hole pulling a dead cow with a red tractor. From the west, Mary McHale was coming with a bow saw and a bag of whiskey bottles, searching for sticks for the fire. He could see a huge curtain of hail sweeping down from the mountain as it approached the old Yank and his new girlfriend coming from the lakeside, all heading for the bog hole. They all passed through the crossroads, first McGuire, all engine and black smoke, then Mary McHale, whistling a Delia Murphy tune, then the Yank in a fancy car with the girl, and finally Deane, with an entourage of crows after him. None of them acknowledged each other, silhouetted in single file before the hail shrouded them.

With a cough of black smoke, McGuire's tractor stopped. He disconnected the cow and, one by one, they caught up with him and pushed the big wheels down the hill until it kick-started with a skid in a cloud of smoke. He reversed back to hitch on the cow while they continued on separately. Mary McHale looked back at the Yank's woman and laughed, her mouth open to reveal two remaining black teeth. Soon McGuire passed them out, the cow leaving a smooth shape in the soft mud as a shaft of weak sunlight passed in front of them before it faded halfway up the mountain.

Deane knew what was going on with the Yank; the whole parish knew but nobody would tell him. The girl applied lipstick in the mirror of the old Buick which purred over the ruts in the track until they had to abandon it. She was much taller than him and smoked his cigarettes in a holder he'd brought home for her. She had even developed an American southern drawl in her speech as he insisted.

'I'm sorry', she kept saying between drags on the cigarette, 'it won't happen again', but the Yank would hear none of it. He appeared to pull her behind him but she didn't want to damage her heels so she strutted instead which ignited his rage even more.

'I don't mean to beat you', she kept saying, 'I love you. Don't you understand?'

They all disappeared over the hill to the bog hole and for a while the valley was silent except for the hiss of the wind through the scalded rushes. Soon smoke from McGuire's tractor could be seen as the red bonnet came into view. Mary McHale was with him looking out the back of the tractor at Deane and the girl. The tractor pulled in as the old woman put her arms around McGuire. She laughed hideously as she gaped out at Deane and the girl. Deane kept his head down thinking, of the headage cheque and the huge fry he was planning when he got home. The girl on the other hand delayed as she leered past Mary McHale at McGuire's flushed face. A rush of power coursed through the old woman before McGuire started up the engine and pushed her out of the tractor. He revved past Deane and the girl on his way to the village.

A black cow was eating the wipers off the Buick, chewing the rubber strips before she let them fall from her mouth. The girl sat down on a rock, threw her long red hair back, took a pebble from her left high heel and started laughing. I never thought it would be that easy to get rid of him, she said to herself. Deane swung a right down the hill, past McMillan's and then past Silvester Fortune's, who was out burning rubbish. Deane tried to ignore him.

'Anyone dead?' he shouted at Deane. He knew that Fortune never went out anymore only to get groceries from the travelling shop that passed every fortnight. 'Anyone dead?' he shouted again always greeting anybody heading for the bog hole with the same refrain.

'No', shouted Deane.

'Half the cunts are dead before they die so it hardly makes a difference', Fortune shouted back.

'Did you hear about Tim Ryan, found swinging in the hayshed last week?' Deane said wanting to divert him.

'Ah, he was a bit of a knacker', Fortune retorted. 'Sure didn't he sell me a Friesian cow one time and her two back tits wouldn't write your name on the door of the barn'.

Deane could see the spike of a new moon squinting over the mountain as he pulled himself away towards the valley.

Soon the frying pan was sizzling as Deane washed himself in the sink. He pumped the black bike before mopping the grease off the pan with a slice of white loaf and settling in to the big plate of rashers, eggs and black pudding. A sickle of moon threw a weak shadow as he stuffed the headage cheque into his donkey jacket and sped down the hill to the Stray Dog Inn. They were all there, McGuire, Mary McHale, the girl and the Yank, who made it back somehow and wouldn't believe that the cow ate the wipers.

'It's a want in them cows on the bog', the barman said, 'they need a lick from the Co-op'.

The Mass crowd hadn't arrived yet, all wide-eyed with approval, clutching children who crowded round the fridge for ice-cream, while the men stole into the bar for a half whiskey. They flooded the place for an hour but soon the bar cleared again except for the regulars. Deane's cheque was accepted and he had a bulge of fifties in his trouser pocket after paying off some debts. He peeled off one and bought drinks for the house. A small red-faced man who had always gone to Mass but got drunk every Saturday night started on about the priest's sermon.

'The priest', he said, 'is a very wise man who preached at length about time'. He quoted the priest. 'The clocks go forward tonight, my dear people, which brings me to the subject of time. You can never go back or repeat anything, a day can never be re-lived in this valley of tears', repeated the red-faced man.

'Don't we live every day the same?' asked the Yank.

I can't tell yesterday from tomorrow', said McGuire.

'Who cares?' said Mary McHale.

The girl said she loved the Yank more every day despite his mean ways, to which the Yank reassured her that they would stay in the Great Southern Hotel for Easter.

There was silence for a while. Deane said nothing because he knew that talking about time was useless, like a goose looking at thunder as the Tuam man says, he thought to himself. But he challenged them to re-live the day and take back the time to see if they would change anything. They thumped him on the back and laughed, determined to make better use of the day.

'Respect time', the red-faced man piped up. Deane ordered one for the road as he reprimanded all in the pub, including the barman, for wasting their lives and not living with purpose and urgency.

The Yank decided that they would have to undo all they had done that day which meant among other things going back to the bog hole and retrieving everything. He wanted to know too if the girl would change her ways. They loaded up on McGuire's tractor and headed off in the moonlight. Soon they passed Fortune's bonfire; he was still out turning over the silage cover with a pitchfork. They were singing the Delia Murphy song, 'you'll never miss your mother till she's buried beneath the clay' – Mary McHale leading the chorus. The moonlight gleamed off the bog lakes and the dead animals glowed under the bottles. They helped Mary fill the bag, Deane pack up the sheep and McGuire hitch back the cow. They all loaded up into the red Ferguson cab and retreated back to the Stray Dog from the crossroads. Mary McHale laughed at McGuire, he looked away. Deane dumped the dead sheep at the gable after he got home, threw some whiskey into a cracked china cup, a gift from his mother's wedding, and fell into bed.

Deane woke up late after drink. He threw an arm towards the noise, cleared the top of the locker, finally found the wind-up clock, silenced it. He stumbled downstairs to the hall where a single envelope was floating on a veil of water. It was the Rural Environment Protection Scheme cheque. Fuck, Deane said to himself as he tiptoed to retrieve it. The water was still dripping off the address part of the cheque and was heading towards the region that said two thousand four hundred and twenty seven pounds and seventy four pence. He angled the cheque so that the moisture flowed away from the numerals. Shivering, he squatted for a while until he was confident that the figures wouldn't be blotched. This time the moisture attacked the thousands and the word two succumbed. The wind was swaying the old trees his grandfather had planted in front of the house and the rain was spitting against the cracked glass in the window. He placed the crinkled cheque between two old books his father once read, one entitled *Flowering Plants and Ferns of Great Britain, Volume 2* by Ann Pratt and a book about Michael Collins, written by Tim Pat Coogan. The Angelus bell came booming across the bog and knelled up the garden against the front of the house. Mary McHale was looking in through the bathroom window.

He pulled on some clothes and two overcoats as he trundled up the hill to feed the sheep. There was one dead, caught in rusty wire. He gathered what was left of her and squeezed her into a Net Nitrogen bag. The rain tore into his face as he jumped over the wall and dumped the new bag beside yesterday's carcass. He headed now for the crossroads with the remains of the sheep.

From the east McGuire was pulling the dead cow. From the west Mary McHale was hauling a bag of bottles with the bow saw in the other hand. The Yank too was purring along in the Buick coming from the lake side as the sun played with the hail showers. Soon the girl got out in her high heels and short skirt.

'I didn't mean to', she said and strutted between the puddles. 'I love you', she kept saying.

'Don't you get it? Don't do this to me'.

Mary McHale followed, bent, looking for sticks – 'something to start the fire' – cutting a long branch with the bow-saw now and again, laughing with a low laugh emanating from the essence of her being.

After they trickled over the horizon descending out of sight to the bog hole, the ancient silence fell. Nothing seemed to happen for a long time. The clouds raced up the hills as the driving showers sunk into the saturated bog, the landscape heavy with winters from another time. A hare might have cantered across hidden gullies, but he didn't. Sun rays, like some celestial search light, picked out at random turf stacks heaped high into the sky and then moved on. Only the bleached rushes gave a name to the wind which now and again came from nowhere to scar the silence with what seemed like an echo. Sometimes a gurgle of water from a collapsed kesh would be caught on a strange breeze. Suddenly the mountains were unveiled, their buttresses facing west into the Atlantic, promising nothing. The yellow-green sphagnum was creating bog at its own pace, the ocean's engine churning out new weather to fling fresh colours over the sodden hills as the disparate figurines emerged in order and in single file, as yet silent, like feathers suspended in the claw of time.

The Gentlemen

Between them they had one hundred and five years clocked up in the public service. Looking out from the tea rooms beside the seaweed baths with the two men in her life, she wondered how it had come to this; she with the latest BMW five series, they were both Audi men. Not bad coming from Leitrim and Roscommon you might say but then they were at the top of their class all the way through secondary school and even when it came to university in Galway, they always got honours, she a first class. For Dympna, everything came easy; sharp features, tight waist and a simple rinse made her a believable blonde. Her father, the local primary school teacher, adored his only daughter. At school, she shone under her father's guided approval, so by the time she got to the Sacred Heart School she was already ahead. It seemed another era now – something from a history book, except it was her history.

They were finishing their favourite chowder and discussing the merits of income continuance plans. She wondered why someone hadn't told her about this, it seemed like a conspiracy almost. This place she couldn't give a name to but now a terrible absence had shrouded her life. It seemed now as if everybody else could see where she was going but to her it was a paralyzing fog. She looked across at the two men, their animated discussions about their pensions and when to get out. Padraig insisted that the deal now on offer would only last for another six months and after that they would have to wait until they were sixty. Jim disagreed, said it would be extended and then he would jump. She looked away at the couple across the tea rooms, a child on a high chair, and outside the families trekking up the steep slope from the beach, bathing towels and grannies in tow, deck chairs in the hands of wiry middle-aged men. She remembered her first years here in the seventies with her parents and the nun, her father's sister.

Her father had never been on holidays but his sister was now allowed to stay in a Sisters of Charity convent away from her school for two weeks annually. She chose Foxford. Every year the ritual would come around, her mother would write to Mrs McGowan in St Jude's guest house around Easter and every year Mrs McGowan would confirm that they could have a single and a double room with a spare bed for Dympna. The nun always arrived in Foxford by train. She came laden with three suitcases, school reports and timetables. The convent lay beside the Moy river which drove the mill where the famous Foxford blankets were made. The site chosen by Mother Mary Aikenhead, who on seeing the poverty in the area, decided to develop the mill. Dympna remembered her dad tucking her in under the Foxford blankets and reading her a story before he turned off the light.

Every day her dad would make the journey from Enniscrone to the convent in the maroon Ford Anglia, she always went with him. Nephin on their right always had a cap of cloud on his head, her father would say. She loved the twists and turns of the Moy on its way from Ballina to Foxford, especially when he went the back road along the foot of the Ox Mountains. Sometimes they would stop to see the fishermen up to their waists in the river in green waders at a long sweeping bend in the river. The nun was always ready when they arrived, already half-way through a rosary with the big brooding habit over her head which rubbed against the roof of the car and blocked Dympna's view of Nephin on the return journey.

Dympna watched the sunlight angle its way into the far recesses of the tea room as the crowds began to trek away from the beach. Jim and Padraig always dined at the Atlantic Coast – a new four star that boldly overlooked the sea, built under the Seaside Town Tax Incentive Scheme. They had their favourite table in the Lighthouse restaurant reserved for eight o'clock. She knew that menu so well, she knew what they would choose and the bottle of house red, French, they would sip and eventually order another before the night was out.

She thought again of the nun perched in their only deck chair on the beach, a rug around her knees reading her Office, her father putting on his togs behind the dunes, her mother later reciting prayers with the nun. Her father would run into the water with her but he never learned to swim. Enniscrone was cold, facing north towards Donegal, but in a light southerly breeze it was almost perfect.

She remembered too wandering off one day when her mother wasn't talking, on those days her dad didn't seem to care. Gone for hours. When she returned nobody noticed. She had walked all the way to the Moy estuary where the north wind whipped the river current. There she watched the choppy waves as the brown water of a sudden summer storm pushed its way into Killala bay. There was a man fishing at the point and the bonnet of a Volkswagen sticking out where it had sunk into the quicksand. The sand blew into mesmeric waves between her toes and gathered in piles behind her. Little dry wheels of spume like demented crabs scurried with the wind towards the dunes. She climbed the highest dune and descended to what is called the Valley of the Diamonds. There she saw a man and a woman on top of one another, with some cider bottles strewn in the sand beside them. After a short time the woman put her skirt on and walked away. The man lit a cigarette. The woman left quickly over the edge of the dune.

Jim and Padraig had parked their Audis on the footpath outside the Atlantic Coast the night before. The waitress had warned them that the new traffic warden might give them a ticket. They explained the new traffic bye laws to Dympna in great detail as they left to park the cars somewhere the fifty cent charge didn't apply.

'Are ye going for that walk ye promised?' Dympna shouted after them.

Jim came back to reassure her that they would be back on the beach at six. Dympna needed to stay on the Operation Transformation regime, four weeks into it she had lost eleven pounds but she could never keep it off. Jim and Padraig were always encouraging. They never had a problem cycling fifty miles most weekends – bikes on the roof. Then there was the hill walking, every hill in Ireland climbed. They had conquered Snowdon and Ben Nevis, the Sierra Nevada in Spain now beckoned. She listened as they plotted the sun holiday in Malaga, the cheap flight from Knock, late spring the time to go before the big heat and after the last snow had melted.

They brought the Audis down to the grass near the beach, Jim's, a black shiny model only months old, Padraig's a two-year old with less brake horse power. Padraig knew his place by now, it had been decided after Jim's promotion ten years previously. Dympna never looked for promotion, she got there seamlessly, and now she was in charge of the department. She never knew the hierarchy, from Passat to Audi to BMW. She just bought a sporty merc, like she bought a leopard-skin handbag in Macy's whenever she took an impulse.

She thought a lot about Jim that summer, he seemed to be a winner. She wondered why they hadn't worked out after college, eleven years living in Dublin beside the sea, long walks and two holidays every year. He was carefree then, too young for playing house he kept saying. She never told him about the miscarriage. He hadn't wanted it anyway. After Jim she buried herself in work; it was the only thing that made sense, something she could control. She met a few men on holidays with her friends but she couldn't make anything happen.

In her forties suddenly she met Padraig at work; he came in every Friday as part of the new inspectorate to monitor hospital performance. Initially he threw his weight around and demanded weekly testing from the lab but she, knowing the legislation, provided the monthly test results with the relevant clause highlighted in the act enclosed by return. Soon they came face to face but she politely rubbed his face on the floor. It had never happened in such an adroit manner and kept him wondering did it really happen. Padraig was different to Jim, reliable, a bit plodding but with him she could see a future. They had tried for a child but it was too late. He so desperately wanted it and soon it seemed that it was the only thing the relationship was about. He moved on to meet Marie and had two children but that didn't work out.

So here they were, she thought, another seaside town with another summer ahead of them, waiting for life to kickstart them. It was strange how they all had become friends, Jim and Padraig, rivals in Galway. She had got to know Jim through the rugby. They'd all become so polite now, never any arguments, but she wondered about the jealousy. Men, she thought, all they think about is career and cars, then it's family. They want the whole package fast, then it's apartments abroad and now it was lump sums, cholesterol and prostate glands. She wanted them to feel something, be angry, sad, something. All they seemed capable of expressing passion about was parking bye laws.

Out over Killala bay the long June evening spread its confident light. The chill had finally gone from the air after an endless winter. People kept saying to each other how good it was to be alive on a fine day and it was, Dympna thought, it's great to be alive to witness another summer. She felt grateful just to be able to share this simple fact with strangers as if it was a discovery. Sometimes it seemed she had more in common with them now than she had with the two men in her life. In her early years, she didn't see patients as ordinary people. They were numbers who had to be dealt with, and they seemed impatient, demanding, with too many kids. She felt like saying, well why do you have so many kids, but she knew in the public service telling the truth could cause her to lose her job. Now she saw their vulnerability more and more since her niece died.

She thought again of the nun and all the novenas said on the way to and from Foxford in the Ford Anglia as she observed puffs of cloud from Nephin heading east towards Ballina like smoke signals for eminent rain. She could see the shiny corridors in the convent and the echo of nuns scurrying to and from the chapel, the tea and boxes of biscuits and her mother's approval when she refused to take one.

'They say children should be seen and not heard but we can't get a word out of this one', the mother superior beamed at Dympna in front of a gaggle of nuns as they fussed over her.

Her dad always winked as if to say take no heed of them crowd. She was glad to escape to the dunes and the possibility of seeing lovers or just to watch Nephin to see what mood it was in that day.

The lads were back at six as promised, all ready for the walk. The tea room had emptied without Dympna noticing and the waitress had the place mopped and the tables cleaned – she had been drinking cold tea for an hour. She didn't really want to walk now; in fact she didn't really want to be with anyone. A strange urgency to go to bed overtook her, she wanted to forget or to get drunk alone, but they were waiting, jumping up and down with that stupid smile reserved only for those who excel in running mindlessly she thought. In her eyes it was a fairly shallow business meriting twenty minutes every day and as little thought or analysis as brushing one's teeth. She looked at them again and wondered what she was doing here in a cold seaside town, staying in a single room, listening to talk about cars and pensions. All she wanted now was to talk to other people; the ice-cream man and praise the day, the waitress about her boyfriend, the barman about his mother. Anger with herself coursed through her veins, to be with these two men who would soon retire but who had stopped living sickened her. She wanted to bang their heads together now but the waitress ushered them into the street and the blinding sun. Jim's dancing up and down irritated her. Padraig seemed defeated, older recently for some reason.

The tide had come in suddenly but they were determined to get to the Moy estuary before the sand was covered. Jim was running back and forward, punching the air in some kind of defiant middle-aged display. She felt cold and old. Padraig was looking out to sea totally disconnected. Dympna looked at Jim with disdain, she wondered now who she was when she loved him. Padraig walked in front of her. Anybody watching would have seen three strangers. Far off, Nephin had its cap on for the night, as her father would have said. She wished he was there now to wink at her about the two lads, as if to say don't take them too serious, to wink it all ok. But now he was in St Benedict's, talking to himself about his teaching days. About now the nurse would be wheeling him down for his medication before parking him at the big table where they all listened to the bingo results on Mid-West Radio. She hoped they would change him before the night.

The water was up higher now than she had ever seen it, so that when they passed the Valley of the Diamonds dune there was nowhere to go but into the spiky marram grass. Jim was still jumping in some sort of bravado theatrics, getting wet and shouting. When they got to the estuary, they noticed something at the edge of the water moving.

'Padraig', she shouted, but he had gone into the dunes.

'Jim', she shouted, 'look, the seal'.

The seal was lying flat on its side but couldn't move. She saw its eyes barely open.

'Do something', she shouted at Jim. He ran up to it but dismissed it, saying it probably came ashore to die. She ran to look for Padraig who was alone in the dunes with his head in his hands.

'Where were you? I need you now'.

She pulled him down to the seal.

'Do something', she shouted at them. Both men knew what this meant. Jim took out his smartphone and dialled Seal Rescue. Bank holiday answering machine he pleaded with Dympna. Padraig swung his coat at the seal but it hissed and attacked the coat. Jim saw a fisherman at the point and demanded that he help them.

He shouted back 'more fish for us guys'.

Padraig again took a timber post from the dunes and prodded the angry seal. It snarled again before hissing.

'Leave him there', Jim said, 'he'll float when the tide comes over him. He'll tear you, he's not worth it'.

She looked back at Padraig who kept prodding him with the post in vain.

'Do something', she pleaded, with open arms at both of them.

Jim noticed in the distance a crowd gathering, waving coats in the air. He could hear distant shouts. He gazed but couldn't understand why they seemed to be shouting in their direction. Padraig looked up from the seal but he too was perplexed. She knew already, she always knew. She smiled up at both of them.

'Gentlemen, it's your cars, too mean to pay in the car park', she smiled.

By now Jim was running.

'Wait, take my keys', Padraig shouted after him but he wouldn't stop.

She watched the two men, Padraig torn between the seal, her concern for it and the car; Jim almost half-way to his new Audi. Something changed in her just then, something she craved all those years. How could she have not seen this before now? Or was it that she wasn't ready to see it? Jim the winner always over Padraig, but he was losing now with every step he took towards the crowd.

The seal at this stage had retreated further towards the dunes and appeared to be dragging itself on one side. Dympna turned her attention back to the seal after what seemed like an eternity. Padraig started cursing the seal and ran after it with his coat; she too was angry with the seal and waved her red leather jacket at it. Padraig wrapped his Crombie coat around the seal's head somehow and dragged it by the tail down into the choppy estuary water where it freed itself in a frantic snarl and flapped its way into the sea. Dympna beamed with delight, ran towards Padraig and wrapped her arms around him.

'Easy', he protested, but she wouldn't be.

Soon she slowly let go a little and eased her grip just enough to allow their faces meet. She didn't need to ask herself what to do next, of this she was sure. Padraig too loosened himself and felt something different coming from her, something definite and simple, something he never felt from her before. He allowed her to make the statement as their lips met before reciprocating. He felt that something was changing, that all those hurdles he could never possibly jump had melted away. They pulled apart but stayed close.

She looked towards where the seal was but all she saw were the squinting sunrays coming across over Bartraw Island and beyond the old Japanese Asahi factory. She was suddenly cold. The tide seemed to be retreating and the wind had calmed down as the night approached. They walked slowly towards the cars. They could see the sun reflecting off the two windscreens. The tide had thrown up clumps of seaweed and pink floats from fishermen's nets. They walked on the wet sand between the high tide mark and the water, touching now and again. Soon they could see a figure running towards them. Jim was out of breath.

'The salty water it didn't get into the engine, it was only inches away, that much', he opened his thumb and forefinger, 'the bad news though is it's in the car. Got in through the doors. The tide will be gone out far enough to move them in twenty minutes, then we'll know the damage for definite. Pity I didn't have your keys', he said to Padraig, 'I could have bailed it out before it got into the seats'.

She looked at Padraig but he didn't seem to care, Jim didn't notice.

'If it was a Toyota', Jim said. 'I'd say she'd be a write off but the Germans they think of everything. The exhausts are very low in all them Japanese yokes'.

'What about the BMWs', Dympna asked as she looked at Padraig.

'My next car will be a Beemer. That's for definite', Jim said. 'I want to park her outside the church in Boyle. That will knock the talk out of them, one like your merc, Dympna, but with black sports wheels, the lot'.

Soon they were nearing the cars, the crowd slowly retreating. Jim flicked his central locking button on the key, all the lights came on. Padraig pointed his, nothing happened. Jim suppressed a smile, sat in and revved up his engine to clear out any water that might have got into the exhaust. Padraig eventually opened his door with the key and noticed Dympna waiting at the other door. She could see inside, CDs, pens and children's photographs floating on her side. She was determined to stick her feet into the water and sit on the wet seat. Jim by now had reversed his car to where Dympna was standing, assuming that she had no choice. She waved at Jim saying.

'Don't be late for dinner now'.

He had the door open.

'Bar food in half an hour at the Lighthouse. See ya there', she pointed towards the restaurant. He quickly pulled the door closed. She watched him drive away.

Padraig couldn't open her door and being a gentleman rang Jim to come back and collect her.

'But it's swimming', he protested.

'I can see that', she said as she eased the mobile away from his ear.

'There's no need to have me rescued', she insisted. 'I'm a big girl now'.

'You can't sit in there', he pointed to the floating sandwiches and CDs but she pushed him to one side, pulled herself past the driver's seat across the handbrake and onto the spongy mess of the other seat. He watched as the water soaked into her skirt and tights. As the sandwiches and biros bobbed between her calves she hitched up her skirt above her waist, smiled and whimpered a high pitched plaintive, 'hi' into him.

'Jesus Dympna, for Christ sake for an intelligent girl …' he threw at her, because he knew this was what he was supposed to say, but secretly he wanted to take her there and then beside the reduced to clear ham and cheese sandwich floating between her legs. She knew him, what he liked and knew that it was money in the bank for later that night. He quickly got in, flustered and drove to the hotel in first gear.

'That bloody seal has infected your brain', he laughed.

They limped past reception to the smiles of the girl and retreated to their separate rooms. Jim was already in the bar pleading for food. The manager conceded to make club sandwiches and chips for three. When Padraig and Dympna entered the bar together Jim refused to see what was happening.

'They'll give us a club sandwich, it's on me, good job I know the manager's brother or we'd be stuck in the chipper eating Chernobyl chicken'.

Padraig and Dympna sat together while Jim kept on talking, trying to deflate what was happening. The crowd was watching *The Sunday Game,* Pat Spillane insisting that Mayo didn't have what it takes. When pressed he said.

'Plenty of talent but they were all too nice, when it comes to any serious game, gentlemen are useless, you need fellas with a killer instinct', he insisted.

Soon the bar closed but not before Jim ordered two rounds of gin and tonics. By now Dympna was silent but Padraig threw back a few words every now and again at Jim who had an endless flow of language as an armory against the imminent silence. By the end of the night Jim excused himself, knowing that it was useless fighting the humiliation. Dympna made no effort to hide her contentment. Padraig suppressed his triumphalism, something he knew Jim wouldn't do.

'Remember tomorrow, up early for Nephin, it's supposed to rain in the evening', Jim warned.

Dympna and Padraig left soon after, she settling into the idea of another beginning. It seemed strange at 55 to be sure. It happened to others at 25 she thought. She felt sad suddenly, for all the things they could never do. In some strange way it could be only a deep friendship now, lived out in a remaindered life for she was by now who she had become while she was waiting for something to happen.

About the Author

Ger Reidy was born near Westport, Co. Mayo. He has won several national poetry competitions and has been the recipient of a number of bursaries and residencies from the Arts Council and Mayo County Council. Dedalus Press published his debut collection, *Pictures from a Reservation*, in 1998, and his second collection, *Drifting Under the Moon*, in 2010. His third collection, *Before Rain*, was published by Arlen House in 2015 and was shortlisted for the Pigott Poetry Prize at Listowel Writers' Week. His poetry has been published in many literary journals, both at home and abroad, and he has read at numerous literary festivals. Since 2012 Ger has judged the Westport Arts Festival poetry competition.

Acknowledgements

Thanks to Mike McCormack, Ian Wieczorek and Alan Hayes for their editing work; and to the Tyrone Guthrie Centre, Mayo County Council and the Linenhall Arts Centre, Castlebar. Many thanks to Dermot Seymour and to Alice Maher.